"Twelve strong stories of science fiction, fantasy, dark fantasy, and horror."

— Ellen Datlow, *The Best Horror of the Year, Volume 2*

"Lalumière's astounding imagination has birthed entire worlds for each story. . . . If you're hungry for original genre content, *Objects of Worship* is just the nectar you've been praying for."

— *Rue Morgue Magazine*

"Freaking awesome!"

— *The Left Hand of Dorkness*

"Takes us on a journey of the weird. . . . A most engrossing and disturbing collection."

— *The Novel Blog*

"Twelve superb and sometimes quite disturbing stories . . . a great collection and I strongly recommend it for every lover of literate speculative fiction."

— *Fantasy Book Critic*

THE DOOR TO LOST PAGES

CLAUDE LALUMIÈRE

ChiZine Publications

FIRST EDITION

Introduction © 2011 by Paul Di Filippo
The Door to Lost Pages © 2011 by Claude Lalumière
Cover artwork © 2011 by Erik Mohr
Cover illustrations © 2011 by Astrid Mohr and Estelle Mohr
Interior design © 2011 by Corey Beep
All Rights Reserved.

Library and Archives Canada Cataloguing in Publication

Lalumière, Claude
        The door to lost pages / Claude Lalumière.

Short stories.
ISBN 978-1-926851-12-9

      I. Title.

PS8623.A465D66 2011   C813'.6   C2010-907883-7

CHIZINE PUBLICATIONS
Toronto, Canada
www.chizinepub.com
info@chizinepub.com

Edited and copyedited by Helen Marshall
Proofread by Samantha Beiko

Canada Council   Conseil des Arts
for the Arts   du Canada

We acknowledge the support of the Canada Council for the Arts which last year invested \$20.1 million in writing and publishing throughout Canada.

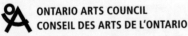

ONTARIO ARTS COUNCIL
CONSEIL DES ARTS DE L'ONTARIO

Published with the generous assistance of the Ontario Arts Council.

THE DOOR TO
LOST PAGES

dedication

For Paul Di Filippo, friend and fellow dreamer, who let me steal the title of his collection Lost Pages.

For Elise Moser, who was there at the birth of the Lost Pages series, offering invaluable support and criticism, and stuck it out through many incarnations and revisions.

For David Pringle, publisher and editor extraordinaire of Interzone *from 1982 to 2004. The fiction and authors published during David Pringle's groundbreaking tenure on* Interzone *had a profound impact on my imagination. That body of literature was an essential landmark in my journey as a writer. In addition, David was the first editor to publish my fiction ("Bestial Acts," in 2002, which would eventually become chapter 1 of* The Door to Lost Pages*); he also published "Dregs" (chapter 3 of this book) and "A Place Where Nothing Ever Happens" (which appears in my collection* Objects of Worship*). Appearing three times in my favourite run of any fiction magazine ever was a dream come true.*

For Miss, Yoda, Golem, Goblin, Kirby, and Konrad; their bestial acts taught me to be a better animal.

CONTENTS

Introduction: His Back Pages, by Paul Di Filippo

His Back Pages

by Paul Di Filippo

When I read and reread the erotic, wise, comic, tragic, passionate, surprising fabulations contained—barely contained!—between the covers of this book, I invariably hear a ghostly accompaniment, that lyrical, endearing croak-warble-whine famous throughout our postmodern world: Bob Dylan, a young Bob Dylan, only twenty-three years old at the time in 1964, singing "My Back Pages," with its famous refrain: "Ah, but I was so much older then / I'm younger than that now."

The stories that comprise this novella—all connected, distally or centrally, to a mystical, mythical (mythical?) used-book store called Lost Pages—embody that oxymoronic, Zen nugget of self-observation by Dylan.

Pretence and pretentiousness, self-consciousness and self-importance, "seriousness," and "maturity," judgmentalism and dogmatism—these so-called "adult" qualities are not the true mark of wisdom or experience in the deep ways of the world. They are instead too often the overreaching, desperately grasping strategies of adolescents and young adults who have forgotten the clear knowledge of pure childhood, but also have not yet attained the hard-won, never-guaranteed insights of older years, which in many ways resemble that selfsame childlike cosmic certitude.

In *The Door to Lost Pages*, Claude Lalumière is intent on showing us that access to one's own heart and soul—and to the coterminous joys of the universe—involves putting down preconceptions and prejudices inherited and inculcated as we age, and returning to the primal source of all wisdom.

The primal source of all wisdom. Symbolized by a shabby, tatty, musty retail establishment named Lost Pages? The omphalos of the multiverse hiding behind the flaking paint of an innocuous storefront? Secrets of true happiness contained in yellowing pages of pulpy or hermetical texts?

Why not? You see, that's the kind of hidebound thinking you have to discard, if you ever want admission to the elect fraternity of *homo ludens*.

In "Bestial Acts," our introduction to this milieu, we witness a kind of lineage transmission, as the current elderly owner of Lost Pages passes on his mantle to Lucas, who has in his own autodidactic way outfitted himself for his new role. Lucas in turn takes the orphaned-by-choice girl Aydee under his wing. Together, they will serve the community of their like-minded peers, of whatever age and race and condition.

We see one of these fellow travelers next in "Let Evil Beware!" Only a child to the world's eyes, Billy is in reality one of the props on which the safety of our world depends.

In "Dregs," our protagonist stubbornly and fearfully resists for a long time the offered transformations that will enhance his native qualities of open-mindedness and curiosity, until a purchase from Lost Pages sets him straight. Or does it? Lalumière never fails to acknowledge that resistance to enlightenment and the potential for backsliding are always possible in the less-than-perfect human realm.

"Dark Tendrils" is one of the few instances where such a failure happens, as missteps are taken and warnings unheeded. It's the necessary black obverse to the ultimately triumphant sense of redemption.

In "Lost Girls," even the wise ones—Aydée in particular—are shown to be utilizing less than their full potential, needing a kickstart to the next plateau in the ceaseless quest for nirvana on Earth.

And finally, "The Lost and Found of Years" puts a classy metatextual spin on the whole package, as author meets creation.

But to say that all these stories embody a similar worldview or set of lessons is not to proclaim them programmatic or tendentious or preachy. Far from it! This fine little book is not some New Age self-help manual: it's involving fiction of the most intimate and passionate stripe!

Claude Lalumière is an adept of prose. His sentences are sprightly and always surprising. His sense of structure is admirable. He plays deftly with horror tropes, fantasy tropes, SF tropes. One minute he's channelling Lord Dunsany, the next Charles de Lint, John Crowley, or Jeff VanderMeer—peers, but possessed of different voices from Lalumière's own unique tones. He braids clues and motifs into a shimmering tapestry. (Just count the sly occurrences of "green, blue, and brown," the colours of a mythical deity.) His characters stalk or dance across the pages, fully alive and palpable.

Additionally, in a smallish but important way, Claude Lalumière is not only a universal author but a regional writer. His native Canada, specifically the city of Montreal, is as much a player in these stories as the people, even when not specifically named. There's some numinous element of these tales that acts as a counterbalance to the hegemony of US fantasy trilogies. We are hearing a voice literally from beyond the lands we (we American readers) know.

I have the honour of being one of the dedicatees of this volume (and even of being namechecked in a story!). It's an honour that causes me to smile with great happiness, to resolve to be worthy of such a dedication, to live up to the ideals on exhibit herein.

I'm still searching for ways to be younger, for the door to Lost Pages myself!

PROLOGUE

Fuel for the Dark Dreams
of Yamesh-Lot

It is said, in one version of the tale, that in those days humanity had taken to burying its dead in the ground. No longer did the people surrender the corpses of their loved ones to the Green Blue and Brown God's acolytes, who would then offer the bodies to their God.

And so did Yamesh-Lot begin harvesting the dead.

From deep in the pit at the heart of the world, Yamesh-Lot's tendrils burrowed into the earth—

far beneath the Godmoat that shielded the world from his darkness—and then back up again, near the surface, careful to avoid the Godpools and the network of underground rivers that connected them. He sought out corpses, found them, wrapped his tendrils around them, and pulled them to him.

Yamesh-Lot poured a portion of his dark essence into each. The corpses grew new eyes: ebony orbs that marked the lifeless, reanimated husks as his.

The enslaved corpses marched toward the subterranean Moon, which rested on its earthen cupule, shielded in the depths of the dark abyss from the ravages of sunlight. They climbed onto the Moon, and there they laboured for their master. Their fragile bodies could not withstand for very long the grind inflicted upon them. Fresh workers were constantly needed.

The workers extracted from the Moon's bowels an ore that Yamesh-Lot forged into weapons: ebony swords that cut through any light and withstood contact with the Green Blue and Brown God's holy waters. He had long envied the swords with which the Shifpan-Shap—those warriors of the Green Blue and Brown God—attacked his nightmare hordes; the dark god's soldiers were too insubstantial to carry such heavy instruments and were thus unable to fight back effectively.

Once the Moon had been stripped bare, Yamesh-Lot raised an undead army that, moonswords in hand, rampaged through the mortal lands of the Green Blue and Brown God while, in the sky, the Shifpan-Shap were occupied by their nightly struggle against the dark god's legions of nightmares. There was a scourge upon the lands as people were set upon by the corpses of their former neighbours, families, and lovers. The world was blanketed by human screams; but even that could not stir the Green Blue and Brown God to intervene directly.

When the moonswords pierced skin and touched human blood, Yamesh-Lot's nightmares finally found a path to the world of dreams. Thus did Yamesh-Lot's tendrils of fear and dread slither into the minds of humanity; finally, the dark god fed on the sweet essence of living mortals; it was a delicacy whose smell had long teased him with its succulent aroma.

But there are other versions, other stories, other outcomes, other delusions, other myths. . . .

CHAPTER 1

Bestial Acts

Now, most of the time, Aydee has no reason to think of the man and the woman. Occasionally, she spots someone walking down the street who for some reason or other—a piece of clothing, a hairstyle, a frown—sparks an unpleasant memory. These are not unwelcome incidents. They remind her that the man and the woman are nothing but a memory to her, that she has succeeded in stepping into another life.

Aydee: that was her secret name, the one she'd given herself. No-one knew of it, especially not the man and the woman who'd given her that other name when she was born.

For the first ten years of her life, Aydee lived in a tiny one-bedroom apartment with that man and that woman. The man made good money. He had a job that required him to wear a suit and tie—he sold something or other, stocks, buildings, insurance, whatever. He shaved every morning, except for the moustache that was much too big for his small face.

Most of the money from the man's job went into business suits and cocaine. The man and the woman rarely slept, rarely ate, and rarely thought of food at all. Occasionally, the man or the woman would order pizza or bring home TV dinners. Even then, she wouldn't get enough to satisfy her appetite.

The woman had the habit of letting small change accumulate at the bottom of the cutlery drawer. Aydee would pilfer it in order to buy lunch at school. Aydee didn't know if the woman noticed that Aydee took that money. Aydee was always careful to leave enough change in the drawer so that it would look undisturbed. Still, she sometimes had enough left over to buy a snack on the way back from school.

Most weekends, the woman would get on the bus to see her mother and bring Aydee along. Aydee and the woman rarely exchanged even a word during these bus rides. Aydee passed the time reading off the street signs, like a countdown to armageddon.

Fat and mean-mouthed, the woman's mother chain-smoked so carelessly that she often had at least two cigarettes going. Every time they visited, the old crone would spew hatred from the moment they stepped in the door to when they left. She'd start with that "no good husband" of her daughter's. Always the same litany: "Did you have to marry one of *them*? They look at you, and all they see is a slave, you know. That's all they'll ever see." Then she moved on to immigrants, neighbours, family . . . she never ran out of spite. While the old crone ranted at the younger woman about this and that, she would serve Aydee platefuls of food: tomato-lettuce sandwiches, homemade cookies and doughnuts, fried eggs and bacon, chicken noodle soup, fruit salad, chicken with gravy, meat pie, apple crumble . . . There was cigarette ash in every mouthful. Still, Aydee ate. The old woman, chiding her daughter for Aydee's thinness, would always insist that they take some food back with them—but that invariably angered the younger woman, who screamed back that she knew how to take care of the girl. It was an argument that the old woman always lost. Aydee knew the old woman didn't really care about her. All she wanted was to dominate her daughter. Aydee was just the most convenient weapon. Every visit resulted in the same fight.

On weekdays, while the man was away at his job, the woman would spend the whole day cleaning, working herself into white-hot rages at the dust and grime that constantly undermined her efforts at spotless cleanliness. She shouted at the dirt in the corners; she screamed at the smudges on the floors; she hissed at the mildew on the bathroom tiles. She could not abide the slightest smear or dust. The apartment reeked of disinfectant. The woman fuelled her fastidious campaigns with a constant stream of cocaine and jumbo bottles of cola.

Aydee had taught herself to be meticulously clean and tidy. Thus, for better and for worse, Aydee was ignored, invisible.

On her tenth birthday, like most nights, the man and the woman were sitting on the living-room couch, watching television with the sound on loud. The one bedroom in that apartment was the bedroom of the man and the woman: a strictly forbidden zone. Aydee was allowed to sleep on the couch, but, often, she was forced to seek refuge in the bathroom. She would take off her shoes and lie down in the tub, inhaling the fumes of the various cleaning products the woman used to keep it sparkling white. That night, though, she just stood in the living room, between the couch and the door, watching the man and the woman. Waiting. Waiting for nothing.

The man was drinking beer; the woman, cola. It was past midnight; the bowl of cocaine on the coffee table was half full. They would still be up for hours, Aydee knew. They might even stay up all night. She was hungry and tired. In the fridge, scrubbed to an immaculate white inside and out, there were only more big plastic bottles of cola and cans of beer. She had tried to drink these before, but the beer smelled like piss and the soft drink felt like exploding sludge.

Her heart was a tight mess of knots, a heavy weight in her chest. She didn't cry. She never cried.

She was hungry. She was tired. Enough; she'd had enough. There was nothing for her here.

She was ten years old, now. She didn't need to sneak out.

Once, I was a ten-year-old boy. Father. Mother. No siblings. No pets. I begged again and again to get a dog or a cat. But my folks were firm on this one. Mom hated animals. She was scared. People can be so stupid.

The best thing my folks ever did for me was leave me alone. On days when there was no school—the whole summer in fact—I'd wander around the city, and sometimes even a bit beyond. Walking. Riding my bike. Taking the bus. Getting on the subway. The city itself was my best friend.

I never made any friends at school. I wasn't picked on either. I was weird, but invisible. I'd learned early on to keep my weirdness to myself. I still remember the first time my mom pleaded with me to act normal, to stop embarrassing her by saying weird things no-one understood. I was only three years old. She didn't threaten me, but the more she nagged me the less connected I felt not only to her but to everything around me, the more I retreated into my imagination. What was it about me that caused her so much distress? Was I really that different from the other kids?

It probably took her and my dad a bit over a year to begin to suspect how far I was roaming. They thought I was just playing outside—in the alley, or in the park down the street.

They made a big fuss at first. They yelled at me, something they rarely did. They made some sort of half-hearted attempt to restrict my comings and goings. For a few weeks they diligently watched over me. They demanded a strict accounting of my time. I was furious for a couple of days, mainly at the realization that they could exert such authority over me. I figured they couldn't keep that up for very long. I was right. It was clearly more taxing for them than for me.

That was around the time I turned ten. Around the same time I discovered books. Looking at me now, you'd think I'd dropped from my mother's womb right onto a messy pile of old, lurid paperbacks and arcane leatherbound tomes. But there were no books in the house I grew up in. The only books I remember from my early childhood are schoolbooks and dictionaries. Except . . . in fourth grade, there was an incomplete set of an old, battered encyclopaedia on top of an old filing cabinet in the back of the classroom.

Aydee was cold. She was feeling faint, hunger and exhaustion getting the better of her. She didn't think to beg for assistance, food, or money. Nothing in her short life had led her to expect help from anyone.

She walked through the streets of the city. There were well-dressed men and women stepping in and out of cars. Brash young folk, not so well-dressed, hurried from here to there, or nowhere to nowhere, huddled in groups, hooting and shouting. In the doorways of businesses that were closed at this time of night, she noticed people wrapped in tattered blankets. Some talked to the passersby who ignored them; others faded into the shadows. Some were very old, older even than the woman's old mother. Some were younger than Aydee.

No-one noticed her.

It was getting harder and harder for her to keep her eyes open. Her legs rebelled against her aimless wandering, urging her to stop and rest.

Aydee ducked into an alley where the intrusive glare of the city lights was diminished. Her back against a wall, she let herself sag to the ground and shut her eyes.

She was quickly able to ignore the city's noises, letting her body slip into the drowsiness that precedes sleep. Then, another sound reached her ears. Purring. It grew louder, until it seemed to occupy all the space inside her head. The more she listened the more complex the purring grew, like layers of sound rippling into each other. Aydee could not ignore the sound. It nagged at her.

The purring came from deeper in the alley. Reluctantly, she propped herself up and walked, slowly, toward the source of the sound. She was so hungry. Every step intensified the pain in her gut. Her eyes adjusted to the dimness of her surroundings. All around her, between the two walls that defined the alley, were layers of rotting garbage: disintegrating bags spilling their contents on the ground, metal cans overflowing, dumpsters dripping foul liquids. There was distressing movement beneath the strewn refuse. Aydee continued toward the sound.

Walking became a trance state. The purring subsumed everything.

Aydee was yanked out of her daze by strong animal odours. The noxious smells of garbage were gone, as was the trash itself. The alley couldn't possibly be as long as the distance she had walked. Could it? Where was she? Suddenly, a short distance in front of her, there was the source of the purring.

A gigantic lioness, almost as big as a whole room, lay on the ground, blocking any possible progress down the path the girl had been following. As Aydee approached the beast, she noticed that all kinds of cubs, pups, and kittens were huddled against the giant's body, playfully intertwined, many of them feeding, blissfully sucking on the creature's teats. Others were climbing, sliding, or sleeping on her gargantuan frame. Aydee felt the hard knots around her heart not untangling themselves but, at least, relaxing some of their relentless pressure.

The giant creature turned her head toward Aydee. The lioness's gaze penetrated the darkness and found its way deep into Aydee. Once more, Aydee felt the knots around her heart loosen—enough so that powerful sobs erupted from a long-neglected part of herself. A torrent of accumulated pain and sorrow gushed from her eyes.

Aydee staggered toward the lioness and nestled amongst the varied assortment of young animals. Her mouth latched onto a free teat. She sucked hungrily, sating needs and cravings she couldn't articulate.

Aydee fell asleep, enveloped by bestial odours and comforting warmth, her mouth fastened on a nipple.

I spent as much time as I could leafing through the pages of that encyclopaedia. I hurried to finish the class assignments so I could have an excuse to go to the back of the class and lose myself in its pages. The teacher was more than happy to see one of her flock eager to spend time reading.

I used to grab a volume at random and let the pages fall. When the pages had settled, I'd look at the open spread . . . the bold headings, the black-and-white photos, the colour drawings. . . .

Inevitably, some item would grab my attention. Often, I'd be seduced by the artwork accompanying the entries describing mythical beasts. Every entry had at least one cross-reference: an epoch, a country, a civilization, an author . . . I'd hunt down the cross-references, trying to put the pieces of these interlocking puzzles together. I still remember the intense frustration I felt every time I failed to find a cross-reference because it wasn't contained in the surviving volumes. A lot of pages were missing, too. Ripped out. How could anyone do that to these books?

I made no distinction between history and mythology. Troy and Gilgamesh, for example, cross-referenced to both historical and mythological entries. Bored and restless and wanting to believe anything that would stimulate me, I was more than happy to accept that these often contradictory readings of the past were all equally true, that reality was not flat and linear, but complex and multidimensional, allowing for many versions of the same events to exist simultaneously. For many pasts to lead to the same present.

Many of the entries in the encyclopaedia were about things that weren't mentioned anywhere else. Things, it seemed, no-one had ever heard about. Like how the dark tendrils of Yamesh-Lot, the lord of nightmares, preyed on humanity's dreams. The exploits of the Shifpan-Shap and their tragic, ultimate curse. The mysteries of the Green Blue and Brown God. Many of these interrelated myths contradicted each other, but that excited me even more. They hinted not only at alternate pasts of the world but at an altogether different way of apprehending reality.

One evening at dinner, I can't remember why, I started to talk about my theories on history, myth, and reality. Maybe somebody had said something that triggered a connection? More likely, I was just eager to blurt out whatever was on my mind.

Before I'd gone very far in my monologue, my parents started interrogating me, angrily, almost viciously, about the origins of these ideas. Where did I find out about such things? Who was putting this nonsense into my head? Who? Who was I spending my time with? Who was telling me these things? Who! Why! Where! How! Why couldn't I be like other kids? Tell us! Tell us! Tell us who's putting all these ideas into your head! Tell us who's making you crazy!

It was Dad who did the most of interrogating. Mom mostly cried. Usually, Dad didn't seem to care as much as Mom about the fact that I was a weird kid. As long as I didn't get into trouble, and I rarely did. But, that evening, he was livid. His face was red. He was lashing out at me, as if I'd done something to hurt or betray him.

I knew better than to talk about the encyclopaedia. I knew—I just knew—they'd arrange to have me banned from reading it, or have it taken away entirely. I screamed that they were my own ideas (they were—but my sadly unimaginative parents could never believe or understand that); I bolted out of the kitchen and locked myself in my bedroom. From that point on, I knew I would never—could never—feel connected to these people.

After that, I still spent as much time as I could devouring the encyclopaedia. It was no longer with the mad rush of a new passion, but with pleasant familiarity. I paid a different kind of attention to the volumes. I examined them not only for their content, but also as objects. I studied the wrinkled spines and scratched covers, ran my fingers over the subtly embossed letters forming the words of the title (*The Clarence & Charles Old World Encyclopaedia*) and the name of the publishing company (Kurtzberg, Vaughn & Jones, Publishers). I carefully memorized all the letters, digits, and symbols on the copyright page.

Around that time, I was spending more time exploring the downtown core. It had never occurred to me before that were such things as bookshops. I was so excited when I discovered that there were dozens of them in the city. I was sure, now, that I'd finally lay my hands on those missing volumes of *The Clarence & Charles Old World Encyclopaedia*.

I scoured all the bookshops. I had no money to purchase the books, but I didn't let that interfere with my quest. I'd deal with that, somehow. But. . . .

I couldn't find the volumes. Frustrated, I started to ask. Mostly, I was curtly dismissed, my query not taken at all seriously. A few times, though, some shopkeeper or clerk would take pity on me and actually look through thick volumes for the title or the publisher. But there was no trace of the *Clarence & Charles* anywhere. No-one had ever heard of it. No reference book even listed its publisher. But I made a pest of myself. I kept insisting, even to the ones who were nice to me, that their references were wrong or inaccurate. I knew the encyclopaedia existed. Every school day, I lost myself in its pages.

It took me a few months to think of hitting the libraries. I thought my experience with bookshops had been frustrating. Ah! That was nothing compared to the humiliation and frustration that awaited me in the city's public libraries.

In those days, libraries—all those I went to—were segregated into "adult" and "children's" sections—in separate rooms. Everywhere, the adult section was open to anyone twelve or older, but anyone younger was relegated to the dull purgatory of the children's section, denied access to the adult area. No amount of sneaking, lying, or pleading gained me entry to the adult stacks or, even, to convince the strict, unimaginative librarians to find out for me if *The Clarence & Charles Old World Encyclopaedia* was to be found in the forbidden sections. I got thrown out of every library in town, once narrowly escaping being detained and having my parents called.

When the school year gave way to summer, it meant that I no longer had access to the *Clarence & Charles*. But by then I had found something else.

I was spending a lot of time in an understaffed, overstuffed five-level bookstore. I didn't find the encyclopaedia there either, but I spent whole days sitting on the dirty floor of that huge maze, reading, with no-one pestering me. The place was so filthy. The books were in terrible shape. Pages torn out. Covers missing. Smelly, gunky stains on the pages. But I'd never seen so many books in one place!

On the fourth floor there was, in a dimly lit corner, a row of books shelved so low they were barely off the floor. They captured my imagination almost as much as the *Clarence & Charles*. They were all from the same publisher, Unknown Knowledge Press. They were all paperbacks, and all the covers had a wine-red background with crude line art featuring pyramids, flying saucers, fabulous creatures, eyes in the sky, and all the usual paraphernalia of esoteric beliefs. The series name was boldly plastered on each cover in larger type than any of the individual titles or authors: Strange World.

Unknown Knowledge Press—what a ridiculous name! But, back then, just the right thing to get my attention. These books presented conflicting, contradictory theories concerning the secret history of the world. Perfect fodder for me: I believed in a fluid past where all possibilities were just as likely, just as true. Although I never came across a book in that series that promoted my theory, it seemed to be the only way to reconcile all the divergent histories and beliefs found in those pages. And I believed everything I read. It was all too fantastic not to be true.

Aydee was awakened by a feather falling on her face. It cut her cheek, just slightly, but enough to make her wince. It was a long feather, almost as long as her arm. And sharp. Picking it up, she nicked one of her fingers. Its colour was a shifting shade of green, blue, and brown. Aydee had never seen such an elusive colour. She wiped the thin wound on her cheek with a finger and then tasted her blood.

The smell of rotting garbage reminded her of the previous night, of her journey through the alley, of finding refuge with the lioness. She looked around her and discovered that she wasn't really in an alley. The night before, the shadows had misled her, and she'd ducked into a crevice between buildings that was barely any deeper than it was wide. The lioness had only been a dream, she thought, could only have been a dream. And yet . . . she wasn't at all hungry anymore. She pushed herself up from her bed of garbage bags.

Still holding the feather, she walked out onto the sidewalk. It was morning rush hour. The streets were filled with people and cars. What were those frenzied shadows moving across everything?

She looked up in the sky. A winged skeleton was brandishing a flaming sword against a mass of darkness from which oozed both clusters of tendrils and a tangible aura of menace. The skeleton, whom she thought of as male because of its size, hung in mid-air, his thick wings—of the same ethereal colour as the feather in her hand—beating rapidly. The darkness had no fixed shape. It erupted from a rip in the sky, blossoming in many directions, sprouting tendrils and limbs of various shapes, only some of which were directed toward the winged creature. Sometimes, a dark tendril succeeded, briefly, in wrapping itself around one of the skeleton's limbs. The winged warrior fought back ferociously, wielding his sword at lightning speed, hacking away at his attacker. It was the most exciting thing Aydee had ever seen.

Aydee tore her eyes away from the conflict. Why wasn't anyone reacting to this? Everyone on the street seemed oblivious to the duel raging above their heads.

A shadow fell across her face. She looked up again to see a dark tendril shooting straight at her. She felt a rush of wind as the skeleton swooped down, chopping off the tentacle before it could touch her. It was then that she noticed the leather satchel strapped over his shoulder and across his chest, his free arm clutching it protectively.

The darkness shaped itself into a funnel and

attacked, trying to wrap itself around the skeleton's head. The winged creature's sword cut through the oozing mass.

The skeleton took advantage of the respite in the dark substance's assault and dove, his sword a fiery spearhead, into the heart of his malleable foe. A thick column sprang out of the darkness and swatted the winged skeleton. The swordfighter temporarily lost his balance. More tendrils and funnels burst out of the dark mass, but the winged warrior's sword slashed through the enfolding darkness, slicing ever closer to the spot from which the darkness emanated, hacking away at the oozing mass with increasing ferocity.

The darkness wrapped a cylinder of itself around the skeleton's head. It savagely twisted its opponent's neck, shaking the winged creature's whole body. It enlaced its tendrils around his legs and wings. The entrapped warrior fought blindly, desperately, his sword cutting through the darkness. It sprouted more and more tentacles, each darting out with increased urgency. But the warrior hovered at the heart of the dark mass. Holding his sword with both hands, he plunged his weapon into the darkness.

There erupted a screeching wail that knocked Aydee off her feet. By the time she regained her bearings, it was over. All she could see was the winged skeleton lying on the ground, partly propped against a lamppost, his flaming sword nowhere in sight. Of the darkness, there was no sign.

She ran to the skeleton. She stood over him and examined him closely. Passersby studiously ignored her.

The warrior's bones were badly splintered. His wings had lost much of their splendour. They were now ragged and sparsely feathered, their colour fading. She looked at the feather in her hand. Its colour, too, was fading.

Overcome with compassion, Aydee reached down to touch the fallen warrior. She wanted, needed to help. She whispered: "What can I do? What?"

The eyeless skull turned toward her. His empty gaze fell on the young girl's worried face. The warrior opened his mouth, but the only sound that escaped was a slow, quiet hiss.

I was grateful for the fact that no-one seemed to notice me in that bookshop. In my mind, it had become an extension of my room. It was a private place where reality didn't intrude.

I was scared when someone eventually spoke to me. It was one of the clerks. He was wearing the ugly brown and yellow staff uniform. Adult alert! But, really, he must have been only seventeen or eighteen. Twenty at most. Adult enough for me back then.

"You love those books, huh? I've been noticing you for a few weeks now."

I must've looked like he was pointing a gun to my head. That's how I felt.

He chuckled, "Hey, don't worry, kid. You can read all you want. No-one cares here. The bosses never come into the store. No-one's gonna bother you."

He stretched out his hand. "I'm Alan."

I managed to bring myself to shake his hand. I

immediately felt much better. He shook my hand firmly, making me feel like a real person.

I gave him my name, and we started chatting. It didn't take long for the conversation to become one-sided. I was starved for attention, and here was someone willing to listen to all my outlandish ideas without laughing at me.

I must've paused for breath because Alan managed to say something. "Hey, listen, Lucas, have you ever heard of Lost Pages?"

From his shirt pocket, he whipped out a stack of bookmarks, flipped through them, and selected one. "Here. I've never heard of this encyclopaedia you're looking for, but if any store can find it for you it's this one. You should go sometime. Really." This was a familiar scene for me. Booksellers were always trying to fob me off on one another, hoping I'd leave. In the same breath he quickly added: "Hey, I gotta get back to work. See ya, Lucas. Okay?"

I could see in his face that I'd kinda freaked him out. I was much more than he'd bargained for. He was too nice a guy to be anything but polite, but,

even back then, as socially inept as I was, I could tell
he was relieved to be rid of me.

The winged skeleton raised his arm and, trembling,
wrapped his fingers around Aydee's wrist. Despite
his wounds, he had a strong grip. The fallen warrior
brought Aydee's hand to rest on the satchel he
carried. Then, the skeleton's hand clattered against
the ground. Aydee put the feather across his
outstretched fingers.

She flipped open the satchel and found inside a
thick leatherbound volume. She took out the heavy
book. There were strange characters embossed on its
cover and spine. For all she knew they could have
been the letters of a foreign language, like Arabic
or Japanese, but she suspected their origin was less
mundane. Aydee looked through the book, hoping,
but doubting, that it might point to a course of
action. Was the skeleton dying? How could she help?

Inside, the book was filled with the same sort
of symbols as on its cover. It was no help; she

couldn't understand anything. But then she found a bookmark tucked between the endpapers and the front cover. Printed in English, in the same colours as the skeleton's feathers, it read "Lost Pages"—with a street address and a phone number.

She knew the name of that street. She remembered sitting in the bus with the woman, on the way to the old crone's house, reading street signs through the window. She could recite the name of all those streets, in order. Getting there would be easy.

She was reluctant to leave the skeleton unguarded. But, she reasoned, no-one else could see him, and, if the darkness—or some other threat—returned, what could she possibly do against it?

As it turned out, I didn't even have to ask for *The Clarence & Charles Old World Encyclopaedia*. It was right there on the shelves of Lost Pages.

The tables, shelves, and counters were packed with books that I had never seen anywhere before. Illustrated bestiaries in arcane languages. Histories of places I had never heard of. Theological essays on mysterious religions with equally mysterious names.

And the dogs . . . there were dogs all over the place. Big and fat. Little and furry. Cuddly and goofy. Slobbering, with their tongues hanging down to the floor. Sleeping, with their paws stretched up into the air. And they were all friendly. This place was heaven. Everything I wanted was right here.

I sat down on the floor, hidden (or so I thought) from the old man at the desk. I flipped open a volume of the *Clarence & Charles* that I'd never seen before, and, instead of frantically flipping back and forth, incessantly checking cross-references as I usually did with the encyclopaedia, I started reading on the first page. A brown Lab mutt trotted over to me, sniffed my nose, and put her head in my lap.

Aydee's quest to help the fallen warrior, to find Lost Pages, filled her with a sense of purpose. Never in her life had she felt moved to do or accomplish anything.

She'd existed from day to day. Waiting. Waiting for nothing, because nothing ever changed.

She would find the shop. She would help the warrior. She had to. For the first time in her life she felt needed. She could not ignore that.

She ran toward Lost Pages, hugging the big, heavy book to her chest.

I completely lost track of time. I was harrumphed out of my reverie by the old man, who, standing at the front desk, had been sorting through a pile of books when I'd come into the shop. He was round-faced, with a big nose, a mischievous smile, and a thick, grey beard. He was wearing the trademark "old bookseller" cardigan.

He was holding a stool in his hands. He put it down close to me and sat. Several of the dogs came to see what was going on. All of a sudden a bunch of them were sniffing and licking my face.

The old man clapped his hands, and the dogs

stopped. "I'm afraid we're closing up. You've been reading that book all day."

Uh-oh. This time I was really caught, I thought. There was no way I could pay for this book. He was just gonna throw me out. I wouldn't get away with this again, I was sure. So close. I was so close. I was holding it in my hands!

He laughed. "Don't worry. I'll put the book aside for you. You can come back tomorrow and read some more."

I was halfway back to my parents' house when I realized that I hadn't said a word to him. I'd simply handed him back the book and bolted out. I just ran. Ran all the way to my parents' house and into my bedroom and shut the door.

The shopkeeper looked anxious. He listened carefully to the young girl, all the while petting a large, goofy-looking Saint Bernard. The shopkeeper's other hand was resting on the skeleton's book, which Aydee had brought with her.

"You're very brave. And smart. You did the right thing. I'll close up, and we'll go right away." He shooed out the few browsers who were loitering in the cramped shop and locked the door. "Wait for me here. I have to get something in the back." When the man walked away, the Saint Bernard came up to Aydee and licked her fingers.

The shopkeeper came back holding an oversize child's wagon. "We'll use this to carry him back here."

The Saint Bernard and two other dogs followed them out. The shopkeeper asked the others—the place was bustling with canines of all sizes and shapes—to stay behind. He dug into his jacket pocket and, before locking up, threw a handful of biscuits inside the shop.

He harnessed the vehicle to the two large dogs. The Saint Bernard's companion was a powerful-looking blond Labrador. A small, thin, black terrier mutt—barely larger than a cat—jumped on the wagon being pulled by the other two dogs.

Aydee led the group to where she'd left the fallen warrior. He was nowhere in sight. "He was right here. I swear he was! I swear."

"I believe you." The shopkeeper knelt by the lamppost the girl had indicated. "Look," he picked up something off the ground and showed it to Aydee. "Bone splinters—and feathers."

"But where did he go?" Aydee bent down and carefully picked up one of the sharp feathers. She wanted to keep something to remember him by.

"I don't know. Sometimes there's nothing you can do but try. You did your best."

"Is he—?"

"I don't know. I really don't. Maybe we'll never know. Maybe he'll come back to the shop tomorrow to get the book again. Maybe not."

There was a long, uncomfortable silence.

The shopkeeper began, "I guess I should head—" He stared at the girl's eyes. He wrinkled his brow and scrutinized her.

"You don't have anywhere to go, do you?"

"I—I. . . . No." She started to sniffle. The small terrier immediately ran to her. He jumped up into her arms and licked her face.

The man stood there for a few seconds, pondering, while the girl hid her face in the dog's fur.

"My name's Lucas." He exhaled deeply. "I'm really hungry. Come on, let's have some lunch."

Not long after that, I disappeared from my parents' world.

Despite my embarrassment at how rudely I'd behaved with the old shopkeeper, I returned to the bookshop the very next day. I really needed to get my hands on that encyclopaedia again.

Just as he'd promised, he'd kept the book for me. I apologized for the day before. He thanked me. Then, he showed me a room in the back where I could sit at a desk to pour through the *Clarence & Charles*. Those volumes were big. You really needed to set them down to read.

Anyway, I started to come every day. Mister Rafael—that was the old man's name—allowed me to help him out. Running small errands, shelving, sweeping. I loved it so much at Lost Pages. It's where I wanted to spend all of my time.

At first, I found Mister Rafael's sense of humour a

bit odd, a bit intimidating, but slowly I started to get it. Pretty soon, we were spending our days trading silent jokes while customers moved reverentially through the shop's stock of incunabula and esoterica.

By then, I knew that the shop only occupied the storefront area of Mister Rafael's large house. I had seen enough to know that I belonged here. Here. With Mister Rafael. And the dogs! And, of course, the books. Learning about everything I'd always dreamed about and so much more I could never have imagined. Making it my life's work.

One night, after the shop closed, I told him I had something important to discuss. Mister Rafael didn't look at me the way other adults did. I felt like a person around him, not like an annoyance to be dealt with. He nodded at me with that wry smile of his. "Let's go in the kitchen," he said. "I'll make us some tea." Drinking tea was his answer to most situations.

We sat in silence for a while, but it wasn't awkward. He waited for me to be ready to speak, enjoying sitting around with me. I was never more sure. So I spoke to him. I told him my life's story. I told about how I felt. I stopped short of telling him that I'd come to see him as my father, much more so than the man whose genes I carried. Those words stuck in my throat. But he understood.

No-one at home or at school knew enough about me to trace me here. And, besides, I'd already begun to suspect that Lost Pages wasn't fully tethered to the world I'd come from.

"I was expecting something like this," Mister Rafael said.

I went back to my parents' house one last time. I packed my clothes and came back to Mister Rafael's house. I came home.

He'd prepared a bedroom for me. Two walls were covered with shelves stacked with books, including a full set of the *Clarence & Charles*. There was a big, old wooden desk. The window was open to let in the cool, late-summer night breeze.

Three of the dogs—Verso, Pipedream, and Unit; they're long gone, now—were lying on the bed, wagging their tails. I went over to them. They climbed all over me, wrestling and playing. That—

—sealed it. I've been living here ever since." Lucas nodded, remembering. "Some years later, when I was old enough, Mister Rafael retired and left to explore all those—" Lucas paused, measuring the weight of the next word "—worlds he had only read about."

Aydee waited for Lucas to explain what he meant, but instead there was an awkward silence between them.

Finally, Lucas continued, "He left the shop in my care and still sends me the occasional message. My life would have been pretty desolate without him."

On the table, there was a spread of breads, fruit, and cheeses, on which Lucas and Aydee nibbled while Lucas recounted his story. There were large bowls of dog food and water on the floor. Aydee couldn't keep track of the number of dogs that came in and out of the kitchen to eat, drink, or get their heads scratched.

She said, "Lucas . . . what happened today . . . does it . . . does it happen often? Is this what your life is like?" She wanted to ask him why no-one else could see the skeleton fighting the darkness. She thought of the lioness, and of learning to trust Lucas enough to ask him if he knew about her. Soon.

"No . . . not often. . . ." He winked at the girl. She giggled.

"Hey! I should get back to work. I've got boxes and boxes of books to sort through." He downed some apple juice. "Wanna help?"

She nodded. Before she could stop herself, she blurted out, "My name's Aydee." She felt scared and exposed, speaking that name aloud for the first time in her life.

"Well, I'm happy we met, Aydee. I really am." When she heard Lucas say her name, she knew she'd come home.

The giant lioness's powerful paw shattered the front door of the apartment, which opened into the living room. She walked in, destroying the doorframe, bringing down the wall.

The lioness strolled up to the couple on the couch—a small-faced man with a big moustache and a woman drinking from a jumbo-size bottle of cola—crushing everything in her path. The couple was oblivious to her presence; they looked right through her, didn't notice the destruction. A thundering growl erupted from deep within the creature. She raised her paw again and, in one swipe, killed both the man and the woman.

Blood and gore seeped into the spotless couch, splattered against pristine surfaces, dropped on the soft, clean carpet.

She sniffed at the corpses. She devoured the stomachs and innards first. She stripped the meat from the bones. She chomped down on the skulls and chewed out the brains, the eyes, the tongues. She shattered the bigger bones with her teeth and sucked out the marrow.

Her meal finished, she left.

Her engorged teats cried for release.

There were many who needed her.

CHAPTER 2

Let Evil Beware!

Billy was eight years old.

He was sitting at his desk in class. The teacher was talking. Billy was looking very attentive. In truth, he didn't hear a word of what the teacher was saying.

Monsters! His head was filled with visions of monsters. He saw himself hunting bloodsucking fiends, flesh-eating ghouls, bone-crushing brutes, would-be world-conquering despotic demons, and snickering creeps who tortured innocent victims. He hunted them down and destroyed them—or at the very least banished them to another dimension.

Let evil beware! None can escape Billy, the monster hunter!

The bell rang and snapped Billy out of his reverie.

It was the last day of school. Billy ran out of the classroom, emptied his locker into his school bag, and hurried out of the school building.

On his way home he stopped by The Golden Age comics shop. It was Wednesday. The week's new comics were out!

"Hi, Bert." Bert was the guy who ran the comics shop. He was tall and friendly, with glasses that looked a bit too small for his head. He played bass in the band Another Grey Truck; as usual, he had on a sweatshirt emblazoned with the band logo. Bert always treated Billy with respect.

He welcomed the boy with a warm smile. "Hey! How's it going, Billy? Last day of school, I hear."

"Finally . . . now I can get back to work."

"Lots of monsters to kill, huh?"

"You bet, Bert. It's frantic work trying to cram in a full load of monster hunting on free weekends and school holidays. It'll be easier now that I can be on the job almost every day."

Billy glanced at the new-release rack. "Wow."

"Yeah, I thought you'd be pretty happy. A lot of your favourites came out today. Here, I put aside the ones I thought you'd want." Bert handed Billy a stack of new comics.

Jade Sentinel. Doc Shadow. Mister Thunder. Strange Tales of the Sproutworld. The Adventures of Kirby & Jack. Baron Nexus. B.E.M. The Preservers. Spiderkid. Rude Dude. Brimstone Kid. The Immortals. The Time Teens. The Detective of Dreams.

"Wow," repeated the awed little boy. "This is great! I can't remember getting so many good comics on the same week." He carefully inspected all the new releases. "Looks like you got everything, Bert."

Billy paid for his comics (his dad always gave him enough money for comics because he read them, too) and headed home.

"Hey squirt. You look happy!" Billy's father was cutting vegetables for tonight's supper.

"Hi Dad! You bet! Look at these!" Billy whipped out his new comics.

"Whoa! You hit the jackpot today!"

"Did you record my—"

"Of course I did, squirt. Why don't you read your comics now? I'll be done here in forty minutes or so; then we can watch the cartoons together."

"Sounds great, Dad!"

Billy hurried to his bedroom and threw his schoolbag on the bed. Clutching his new comics, he went to the living room and buried himself in the couch to read while he waited for his father to join him to watch today's episodes of *World's Best Heroes*, *Chuck Amuck*, *Leave It to Lucky!*, and *Opus the Cat*.

Tomorrow, he thought (flipping back the cover of *Baron Nexus*), *tomorrow I'll hunt monsters.*

"Hi, I'm Billy. I'm here to get my stuff."

It was nine, Thursday morning. Aydee had just opened up Lost Pages bookshop for the day. This was the first time she had done it by herself, and already she felt out of her depth. She'd started the day confident she could handle anything. "Your . . . stuff?"

"You're new here, right? Where's Lucas? What's your name? What do you know about monsters?"

"Hey, slow down . . . Billy," Aydee said, remembering the little boy's name.

"You don't look much older than me. Do you really work here?"

For a moment the two children faced each other down. Why was this annoying kid giving her a hard time? Exasperated, Aydee broke the duel and busied herself tidying the counter.

She sighed, and said: "Yeah, I do. I work here. Listen—Lucas will be back soon." Aydee would be glad to shoo this strange little boy onto Lucas. He should have warned her about him! What else should she know but hadn't been told?

Billy looked around. "He must be walking the dogs, right?"

"That's right."

"Well, maybe you can help me in the meantime." He rummaged through his knapsack and pulled out some sheets of paper.

"Do you know if you have anything on this critter? I think it's a Low Bunny," he pointed at a drawing of a rabbit with giant fangs and yellow scales, "but I'm not sure." He pressed on, oblivious to her anxiety. "What about these?" He indicated a roundish construct made up of smaller, multicoloured spheres. "These, I'm pretty sure, are the Bouncing Balls of Boomworld. Or what about these?" He showed her a picture of naked men and women with rainbow skin. "I have no idea where they come from. Do you?"

Aydee was saved from the barrage of questions by the arrival of Lucas's dogs. They swarmed over Billy, greeting him enthusiastically.

Billy was playfully wrestling with some of the dogs when Lucas spotted him.

"Billy! How you doing? Haven't seen you around for a few weeks."

"Yeah . . . I just couldn't get away. Family stuff, blah, blah, blah."

Lucas nodded knowingly. "Mmm . . . school must be over by now, right?"

"Yeah, I'm free! But I got lots of work to do today."

"Busy dreams last night?"

"You bet! Take a look at these." He handed over his drawings to Lucas.

"You don't usually dream about Yamesh-Lot," Lucas said with concern, inspecting the pictures.

Aydee's blood grew cold at the mention of the dark god's name. Sometimes, she thought it was crazy to stay here, where she was confronted with these kinds of dangers. But then she remembered that when she had almost fallen prey to Yamesh-Lot she had never heard of him or of Lost Pages.

She strained her neck to get a glimpse of Billy's drawing. But there was no detail; only a black mass inside a thick white border.

Billy dismissed Lucas's anxieties. "Don't worry. That border? That means he's still contained. It's all under control."

Lucas nodded approvingly at the boy's words, but Aydee wasn't convinced. Just who and what was this strange little boy? How could he be a match for the lord of nightmares?

Lucas continued to leaf through Billy's stack; he stopped and gasped, and his eyes grew wide. "Are those the Purple Zombie Rats of the Spectroverse?"

"Yeah, looks like they're back."

Addressing his assistant, Lucas said, "Aydee, can you look after the shop alone for a while? I'm gonna be busy in the back with Billy, okay?"

Billy attached the two big pouches Lucas had given him to his bicycle rack. All kinds of sticks and things protruded every which way.

He jumped on his bicycle and waved goodbye to Lucas and Aydee.

Watching the eight-year-old boy ride away, Aydee yelled: "What. Was. That!"

"That, my dear, was Billy, the monster hunter."

"Don't be coy, Lucas! Tell me."

"What can I say? He keeps his monster-hunting equipment here so his parents won't find it, and I help him out with research so he's well prepared when he comes up against the monsters he hunts. What's to tell?"

"Fine. Be that way."

Billy's mother tucked him in. "You know, you really should try to be more careful when you're out playing, my little darling." She gently brushed her lips over the bruise on his forehead.

"But, Mom, two Weredevils from Planet D'tk jumped me from behind while I was performing a rite to banish the Purple Zombie Rats of the Spectroverse. I managed to suck them into the vortex I conjured for the Zombie Rats, but not before they got in a couple of good smacks."

She sighed in exasperation, but the sigh turned into a chuckle. She beamed an amused smile at her son.

"Yes, Mom. I'll be more careful." *But*, he thought, *the Purple Zombie Rats of the Spectroverse are still on the loose! Tomorrow. Tomorrow, I'll get them.*

Billy's mother kissed him on the cheek, rose, and turned off the light.

"Sweet dreams, my little man."

"Goodnight, Mom."

She closed his bedroom door.

Exhausted from his hectic day, Billy fell asleep immediately.

He dreamt.

He dreamt of the Purple Zombie Rats of the Spectroverse (again!) and the Stone Ghouls of the Bottomless Pit and the Fireflies of Doom and the Giant Vampire Mosquitoes of Creepy Island and the Screaming Hulk of Neospace and the Lurking Leeches of the Forbidden Zone.

On the night table next to his bed, there was a fresh stack of white paper and, in a wooden mug, a bunch of well-sharpened colour pencils.

Tomorrow, another busy day awaited Billy, the monster hunter. He would be ready.

Let evil beware!

CHAPTER 3

:

Dregs

Aydee had stepped outside with Lucas and the dogs. She enjoyed the misty not-quite-rain and the faint glow of the morning sun attempting to pierce the flimsy cloud cover. When the weather was like this, she felt the world reflected her sense of place in life: neither this nor that; neither here nor there; perpetually on the brink of transformation; unwilling to settle for just one potentiality. The dogs turned the corner, and Lucas vanished after them.

Aydee dug her fingers into her frizzy hair, the dampness comforting her with unarticulated impressions of a nostalgia for a past entirely different from the one she had known, of a primordial memory of the essential moistness of life. She filled her lungs with the finely humid air, felt the contended smile spread on her face, and turned back inside to open Lost Pages for the day.

She was engaged in her futile morning ritual, attempting to put the perpetually chaotic shelves into at least a semblance of order, when the mail arrived. The mail carrier tended to avoid stepping too far inside the store, habitually leaving the mail on the nearest stack of books without making eye contact with either Lucas or Aydee and knocking loudly to announce the day's delivery. But today a package needed to be signed for, so he nervously approached Aydee, darting a sharp whisper at her: "Signature." The parcel was for Lucas; except for the occasional correspondence still addressed to Mister Rafael, the mail always was always addressed to either Lucas or the shop. Never to Aydee. Even though she worked here and lived here.

Nevertheless, Aydee sifted through the day's mail, curious about the exotic stamps—many from countries that might not even exist, as most people reckoned things. Some of the envelopes were illuminated with strange drawings she could not quite make sense of. But it was a thick, plain, oversize white envelope with mundane stamps and no return address that most attracted her curiosity. It was addressed simply to Lost Pages. Its stark austerity intrigued her, commanded her attention.

She heard the sounds of the dogs coming from near the door. Without thinking, she stuffed the letter inside her clothes just as Lucas burst into the store with his pack.

She showed Lucas the day's mail—minus the purloined white envelope—and, without another word, stepped through to behind the store, to the part of the house where she and Lucas lived. He was so entranced with that parcel Aydee had had to sign for that he didn't notice—or at least comment on—the girl's nervousness.

Aydee didn't know why she'd hidden that envelope. Had she asked, Lucas would have shown her its contents; he wouldn't have minded if she'd opened it without asking first. It wasn't his way to be secretive or authoritarian with her. He might be coy, or have a flair for dramatic mystery, but he never out-and-out hid anything or deceived her.

But she wanted this letter to be hers, and hers alone. She wanted something—anything—to be hers. All this—Lost Pages, and all the wonder that came with it—it wasn't hers. Most of the time, it all felt right, like she belonged here and nowhere else, and certainly not in the world of her nightmares. But sometimes the sensation of being a guest or even an intruder, of this new life being transitional, crept up on her and she would have to fight the panic that threatened to seize her.

Up in her room, she minutely scrutinized the letter. There was nothing to observe. Save for the address of the shop, the envelope was blank and plain. Delicately, she peeled it open and slid out the contents: a thick pile of handwritten pages, torn from a notebook, clipped together with an unsigned typewritten note.

Dear Lost Pages,

I yearn to share this story of my life with someone who will believe me. And I suspect any of you know more of the truth of this tale than I do or ever will. Initially, I thought that writing out the story as a long diary entry would suffice me, but it did not. And so, finally, I decided to send these pages to you.

I need someone to know of, and perhaps even care about, these unusual events that moved me so profoundly—some might say scarred me, but I treasure these memories too much to belittle them so.

Please forgive the anonymity—you will notice that I was careful to avoid names of people and places that might lead to my identity—but this impulse to expose the story of my life does not trump the urge to protect the contemplative privacy that finally allows me a measure of serenity that had long been denied me.

My thanks—for indulging me, yes, but for much else besides, as this tale will make clear to you.

Aydee had to control herself so as not to scream

with excitement. Here was a story she needed to read: an opportunity to learn how other people, besides Lucas, besides herself, had been affected by their contact with Lost Pages. A chance, maybe, to better understand this strange life and her place in it. She bundled herself in her reading chair, enraptured.

According to an old folktale, nightmares once covered the night sky, blotting out the stars. When those creatures of darkness invaded our dreams the night sky opened up, and the stars revealed themselves.

I found the book that contained that particular story at one of my favourite teenage haunts. Lost Pages wasn't the only bookshop I frequented, but the books I found on its shelves were . . . unique. I never saw any of these books anywhere else. Bizarre bestiaries. Dictionaries of dead, obscure languages. Maps to lands that may never have been. Essays on religions with unfamiliar names. Obscure mythologies. Accounts of wars no history teacher had ever mentioned. Such were the wares of the bookshop that fed my teenage dreams. But I left my hometown after high school, when I took my first trip overseas, and, shortly after that, went to university in another city. Lost Pages was left behind—a passing fancy of adolescence.

My parents had offered me a two-month-long voyage abroad for, as far as I could tell, two reasons. On the surface, they felt they could afford this luxury because, unlike most of my graduating class, I showed no interest in automobiles; many of my classmates were rewarded with a shiny, fashionable car for coming out of high school alive. Unspoken, however, was that my mother and father worried that I was spending too much time in my own head. They often commented, with varying degrees of tact and concern, on my lack of friends. They judged—as it turned out, wisely—that being dropped alone in the middle of foreign lands would make me notice the world around me.

And so I did. I stood next to the sea at dawn, inhaling its pungent aroma. I walked through streets too narrow for automobiles, yet bustling with human activity, loud with foreign languages and cacophonies. I ate delicately spiced foods, enjoyed an undreamt-of variety of meats, vegetables, and fruit. I wandered city avenues where lovers danced and kissed in the moonlight to the tunes of street musicians or of their own hearts. And there was so much more that I experienced. This whirlpool of exotica awakened in me unfamiliar lusts.

Two weeks into my trip—on a hot summer night at times tempered by an elusive cool breeze—I was in a port city whose hectic nightlife clustered in a busy quarter next to the docks. Club music blasted through open doorways, mixing with the sounds of outdoor performers. The women wore short, tight dresses, advertising their physical charms to potential suitors. The men, overdressed in the heat as was the fashion, sweated the night away dancing athletically, careful never to let their eyes wander from the women they coveted. I was mesmerized by the nimble performances of these dancers, the precision of their movements, the sway of their hips and shoulders, the sweat spraying from their brows as they swirled to the rhythms of the dance music.

I was tempted to dance myself, but there was no-one I wanted to impress or seduce. It was a notion I could barely contemplate. My new experiences had yet to include sex—I had never even masturbated! The sexual energy that, unknown to me then, was yearning to break free was intensifying the self-consciousness I felt over my awkward body. Not being a fashionable young man, I was dressed to be comfortable in the heat: thin cotton pants and a T-shirt. My awareness of the inadequacy of my appearance emphasized the notion that I was a child among adults; I remained a spectator.

I had been in this city for three days. Each succeeding night, I was further entranced by its vigorous nightlife, by the soulful music, by the simmering sexuality.

As the evening wore on, I grew increasingly frustrated at my inability to join in the festivities. I felt cheapened by my voyeuristic role, and I was tortured by an inner conflict—the desire to abandon myself to the surrounding merriment clashing with an unshakable fear of embarrassment. Burdened with self-loathing, I decided to return to the inn where I was staying, hoping to calm down enough to fall asleep.

On my way back, I was overtaken several times by an extreme dizziness and had to brace myself against walls or lampposts to keep myself from stumbling. I was not tired—quite the opposite! I was a nervous mess: exhilarated at the intensity of my experiences and angry with myself for my cowardice.

A block or two from the inn, while I was suffering another bout of dizziness, my hand failed to find a steady purchase, and I fell. A young man—he looked about my age—rushed to my side to help me. The skin-on-skin contact—my rescuer's hands clasping my bare arms—was such an intense shock that I almost fainted.

I took a deep breath, and, with the stranger's help, I got up and steadied myself. He looked vaguely familiar: slightly taller than I, dark eyes, olive skin smooth and dry despite the heat, strong sharp features, a pronounced nose, stylish black pants and white shirt. I was dazzled by what I took to be a trick of the light: highlights of green, blue, and brown shimmered in his dark hair. Probably I had seen him at one of the clubs, or in the streets among the strollers and dancers.

His gaze locked with mine as he asked me something in a language I could not understand—he spoke so fast I couldn't even be sure which language he was speaking. He seemed genuinely concerned. I tried to mime that I was all right, livening up my risible performance with a few simple English words.

He laughed at my antics. I surprised myself by laughing along with him. I was such a serious young man. Laughing at myself was a novel experience. It somewhat attenuated my self-loathing.

Looking at my companion, I remembered the handsome men dancing to seduce the eager young women watching them. I was overcome with a vision of my new friend dancing as I had seen those men dance: his hips and shoulders swaying confidently, his seductive smile directed toward me, his eyes never straying from my body. . . .

The next thing I knew his lips were closed over mine, his tongue exploring my mouth, just as my own tongue tasted the wetness of his.

I panicked. I shoved him away. The dizziness was

stronger than ever; again, I felt faint, but I struggled not to succumb to this weakness and ran to the inn.

Inside my room, I fell into the chair, closed my eyes, and took long, slow breaths. I was confused, my panicked heart thumping wildly. But I was also exhausted. I got up and started to undress, eager to climb into bed.

Taking off my pants, I was startled by the sight of my erect penis. Of course, I'd had erections before, but I'd never paid any attention to them. This one, huge and dripping, refused to be ignored. At that moment, it occurred to me that I had felt its pull all evening. Nevertheless, out of naiveté and habit and ignorance, I still neglected it.

Why had I never masturbated? Even now, I can't really say. Not out of prudishness, and certainly not out of some strange belief that it could be evil or bad in any way—I simply hadn't.

I crawled into bed, determined to fall asleep—despite my overengorged penis—and put this troublesome evening behind me. Tomorrow, I thought, I would check out and head for another city. I felt compelled to flee. I was too young to know that, no matter how far I fled, I could not escape myself.

The erection made it difficult for me to get comfortable. Nevertheless, I did succeed in falling asleep.

I awoke trembling with violent pleasure, and, before I could take stock of the situation, an inner explosion sent aftershocks of ecstasy rippling through my body. I was unable to make out any distinct sensation. My sense of touch was now so acute that all contact with my skin—air, sheets, anything—contributed to the sensation of being enveloped by a warm sea of delicious comfort, like a fetus blissfully floating in its world of amniotic fluid.

Slowly, I regained the ability to distinguish sensations. I felt my back bathing in a pool of sweat. I felt the cool breeze from the open window next to my bed. I felt a warm mouth around my spent cock.

My fellator was the gorgeous young man I had met earlier in the streets. His kiss had been my first. And now he had given me my first orgasm.

He must have sensed a shift in my posture; he took his mouth off my penis and stood up, examining my face. There was enough moonlight coming in from the window for me to make out his seductive, mischievous smile.

I recalled how he had so easily succeeded in making me laugh at myself. Seeing this strange and brash boy towering over me with his proudly erect cock, I could not help but recognize the comical nature of my behaviour earlier that night. What a burlesque figure I must have cut! Running scared from my own body, from my excitement, from its fulfillment, from my new friend's beauty, from the possibilities his body offered me.

As he smiled at me, I laughed. Instantly, he was infected by my outburst. He leapt on me, and we hugged fiercely, still laughing.

After hours of exploring each other's bodies, we lay silently in bed, my head on his chest while he stroked my hair. The first light of dawn was seeping through the window. He kissed my forehead and disentangled himself from me. I closed my eyes, savouring the lingering sensations of his touch.

I heard him fumble around the room, and, moments later, I felt his hand on my stomach. I opened my eyes to see him offering me a drink from what I took to be a bottle of wine. It was transparent, clearly revealing the amber fluid within.

Seeing me hesitate, he took a sip himself. Overcompensating for my timidity, I grabbed the bottle away from him, more roughly than I'd intended. I kneeled on the bed and, theatrically, raised the bottle to my mouth. I swung my head backward and let the dark liquid cascade down my throat, nearly gagging as a result of my eagerness to show off. Rivulets of amber flowed through the burgeoning hair of my adolescent chest. He snatched the bottle away from me before I spilled the entire contents.

I coughed to regain my breath but found myself dizzy and drowsy. The shapes around me were losing their definition. Once more, my seducer kissed me. His tongue playfully explored my mouth as I felt his fingers gently tighten around my scrotum.

I did not lose consciousness; but my sense of self dissolved into—

Fabulous creatures emerging from exploding stars. I myself am one of many laughing monsters fro-

licking amongst the flames of the sun. I witness great migrations of majestic undersea beasts. I am the great primeval ocean in which they thrive. I undergo uncounted metamorphoses, limbs turning into wings turning into tendrils turning into leaves turning into ripe fruit turning into stone turning into molten lava turning into dark ambrosia trickling down the throats of unfathomable deities turning into a thin old man wracked by ceaseless physical pain turning into a glowing snake changing colour with every flick of its tail while negotiating a path through high and dense grass turning into a pantheon of gods smashing planets asunder for their amusement turning into a stomach growling to be fed turning into a baby suckling at its mother's teat turning into a host of dark shapes writhing in the sky.

I was struck silent, stunned by this torrent of hallucinatory visions—if visions they were.

My companion kissed my chest, and then rose from the bed. He drank the amber liqueur down to its dregs. He looked at the bottle longingly, then bent down to kiss me. I tasted his tears. He carefully positioned the bottle on the night table. Did his feet and hands turn into claws? Did scales sprout from his flesh? Did his moist mouth take the shape of a beak? Did wings with feathers of green, blue, and brown rise tall above his shoulders? Did he fly through the ceiling and into heavens as strange as those I had just glimpsed?

I lay in bed immobile, listening to the furious sound of beating wings.

When I could move once again, I stared at the nearly empty bottle. Were it not for the evidence of that bottle I might have dismissed the events of the last several hours as feverish delusions. No, my erotic adventure had been real enough; the delightful tingling that lingered on my skin and the musky smell of sweat and semen attested well enough to that. But as to what came after I drank the mysterious liquid . . . had my lover slipped me a powerful hallucinogen? To what purpose? Stupidly paranoid, I immediately convinced myself that he had robbed me.

I sprang from the bed in search of my pants. I found my wallet undisturbed. I rummaged around the room and calmed myself down. Nothing was missing.

It would be many years before I made any sense of my bizarre encounter.

I enjoyed the remainder of my holiday more than I had previously anticipated, as I eagerly explored myriad new worlds of taste, smell, sound, beauty, and sex. I returned home only briefly. University was a few days away.

My parents immediately noticed a change in me. I was more alert. My eyes were brighter, and I smiled much more easily. My parents deluged me with questions about my trip.

Ordinarily, I would have fled from such a barrage of attention. But I knew they were only happy to see me, and that they would miss me once I was gone to university. Also, I was very grateful for their gift to me, that vacation that I couldn't have known how much I needed. Of course, I would answer their questions. But I also knew that I could not be entirely candid.

They asked about the bottle I had brought back as a souvenir. I answered coyly that it was to remind me of someone special. They did not press the issue, not wanting to embarrass either me or themselves.

Their thoughts were transparent. They were imagining some exotic girl, nice but not too nice, who had deflowered their shy son. The reality would have shocked them, as, in fact, would the extent of my sexual escapades. So I gave them a nice, polished version of my travels: enough details for them to know that their idea had been a success. But I was also vague enough to let them to understand—by omission—how much of one it had been.

Yes, I had kept the bottle. It was not quite empty. There were some dregs, some few lingering drops. I was both tempted and scared to sample the liquid again. I did not know what to make of its effects— if indeed it had been responsible for my vivid hallucinations—and I was loath to waste what little there was left. I thought of diluting the remains in water. Drinking the results only occasionally, slowly learning to understand the visions it bestowed upon me. It was too soon. I put the bottle away, intending to leave the decision to a later time when I would have the leisure to think properly.

The few days between the return from my voyage and my departure for university went by with alarming rapidity. Did it occur to me at the time to visit Lost Pages? I can't remember—but, even if it had, I would not have been able to find the time to go. And how could I have known what to look for?

To facilitate my preparations, my mother had already packed most of my personal effects. My clothes were neatly folded into old suitcases. My books had already been stored in boxes, ready to be shipped to my dormitory.

In this new life, my time and mind were now occupied with my studies and the string of tedious jobs I had decided to take in order to afford an apartment that would secure me the privacy dormitory life failed to provide. I was discreet and avoided permanent entanglements. I attracted— and was attracted to—those who yearned for an intimacy that would not shatter their daily lives or their other, more public, attachments. Mostly men, but also occasionally women.

I rarely returned home to my parents. They saw me for some, though not all, of the customary holidays and requisite family events. Those visits were short and never included enough time to visit my old haunts. It was as though my previous identity had been supplanted by a new one that recognized no continuity with the past. Everything I had experienced before university—more precisely, before that fateful summer trip—might as well have happened to someone else.

Eventually, teaching assignments supplemented the scholarships I earned, and the two sources of income allowed me to quit migrating between minimum-wage jobs to support myself.

One night a young woman—a mischievous student whom I had met the previous semester while teaching an undergraduate survey class—noticed the bottle on a shelf among other knickknacks nestled between piles of books.

On the floor of my living room, we were naked, the sweat of sex clinging to our cooling bodies. We were laughing at everything and nothing until the laughter escalated into a wrestling match. I had her pinned down between my legs, mercilessly digging my fingers into her ticklish belly, but, in a surprise manoeuvre, she managed to squirm and jump away from me.

She ended up on the far side of the room, staring at the bottle. She called me over to her. "Look at how the light catches." She pointed with one hand and squeezed my buttocks with the other. "It's beautiful."

At the bottom of the bottle, where light hit the amber liquid, miniature rainbows danced. If I tried to concentrate on any particular aspect of this tiny spectacle, it hid from my sight. I had to absorb the phenomenon in its entirety, or not at all.

Why had I never noticed this? Had this effect been going on unnoticed all these years?

How could I know? I had found it simpler to ignore my memento. I suppose I passively cherished its presence, but I had yet to pursue—or even to contemplate pursuing—my investigation of its contents. A council of unacknowledged, intertwined fears sat at the heart of my negligence: that my life of pleasure would be shattered by the revelations awaiting at the conclusion of a successful invest-igation; that there were no answers to be found; that the liquid would turn out to be nothing more than wine or some other mundane beverage; that I had those many years ago lost my grip on sanity and been besieged by delusions; that my great moment of epiphany rested on an instance of madness; that the foundations of my personality were too fragile to withstand close scrutiny. However, these personal insights were still in my future, some time later than that evening, when I stood in my living room, my naked body pressed against my lover's soft back, as we both stared at the contents of my precious bottle.

The dregs appeared somewhat more substantial than I remembered. Hadn't there been but a few drops? There was now a pool at the bottom of the bottle.

"Tell me the story," demanded my lover, tucking a stray strand of her blond hair behind one ear.

"What do you mean?" Unsuccessfully, I attempted to resume our tickling match.

"Stop it! There must be a story! What are you hiding? Tell me. Tell me!"

I had never revealed the story behind this bottle. Except for my parents upon my return from my fateful voyage, no-one had thought to ask.

I had never told anyone.

Suddenly, I felt the tremendous weight of this

secret. In her curious, smiling face, I sensed the potential for release and relief. To finally relate the events that had changed my life.

I must have been silent for longer than I realized. She was gently stroking my chest. I noticed her looking at me, worried.

"Yes," I said.

"Yes?" she whispered back at me.

I led her into the bedroom, and, then, I told her.

I told her everything. My whole life. She listened to my ramblings, paid attention to every word. She never grew impatient—or at least was sensitive enough to my needs not to show it if she did. Somewhere in this great mess of a narrative, the bottle's story came out. I omitted no detail, no matter how utterly embarrassing or unbelievably fantastic.

Why did I trust her so when I had never allowed myself to open up to anyone in this fashion before? Because I needed to. I do not mean to undermine or diminish the depth of her empathy or her curious intelligence, and certainly not the quality of her companionship. No doubt all of these aspects of her combined to trigger my realization of this great need, this great chasm, in my life. My need may not have necessarily been to share with her, but without her I would not have been able to acknowledge— much less satisfy—it.

I can't remember how or when, but my confession segued into sex. There is no clear dividing line in my memory between the two. It was all communion—I thought I understood that word more deeply than ever before. I lost myself in my lover and became one with her.

I also can't remember when sex turned into sleep. One moment I was intoxicated by my lover's smells, our smells, the pungency of our bodily secretions . . . the next I was waking up, languorously serene, to see her eyes scrutinizing my face.

I took her hand and kissed it. "I—"

"Don't say . . . don't say anything. Shh." She placed her fingers over my mouth. Her eyes avoided mine. "Don't."

We had been hugging in silence for a short while when she said, "We should get going. We both have busy days today." I grabbed her wrist and looked at her watch. She knew that my next class was to start in fifty minutes. I prided myself on my punctuality. I would not make my seventy-five students wait.

I was irritated that she knew my schedule. I wondered—silently—about her own affairs. What did I know of her? I became ashamed of myself, ashamed at my selfishness, my egocentrism. Did I ever inquire into her daily grind? Did I ever show any interest in the details that made up her life? I hid that lack of interest under a veneer of sophistication, under the idea that we met not to encumber each other with the boring minutiae of our quotidian routines but to escape into an oasis of sexual delight. But wasn't all that a petty excuse to forgive myself for the lack of interest I exhibited in my friends and lovers? I was such a peacock. I was embarrassed; I now saw myself as a clumsy, transparent, ridiculous jester. As someone whose relationships didn't matter, didn't mean anything. As someone who didn't matter, neither to myself nor to anyone else.

I fled to the bathroom, using the time as a convenient excuse. Any notion of communion had been shattered. I heard her walk around the apartment, heard the clinking of a belt buckle as she was getting dressed.

"Gotta rush! See you soon!" she shouted from two rooms away. In my agitated, self-engrossed state, I failed to fully register the uncomfortable and distant timbre of her tone. I heard the door open and close.

I turned my mind away from introspection and, instead, toward the busy day ahead of me. I washed and dressed in a precise hurry and managed to step into my classroom a few seconds early.

That day was interminable. Illusions had been destroyed, and I was in no shape to deal with the wreckage. I yearned to see her, yet dreaded the prospect. I needed and feared her. Was it brave to stay alone? Was it cowardly to not call her, or anyone? Alone, I could hide from eyes that could penetrate my thin carapace. With a lover, I could lose myself in erotic fulfillment. No matter what I did, I was hiding.

That evening, I was too restless to read or work. I couldn't find any comfort in music; the familiarity of my record collection irritated me, and the radio was intolerably banal. I ate incessantly, stuffing food—raw vegetables, crackers, baking chocolate . . . whatever I could find—into my mouth continuously, as if the slightest respite would allow some unnameable threat to invade my innards.

It was only nine o'clock when I decided to go to bed. Beforehand, remembering the previous night, I felt compelled to walk to the shelf where rested the memento from my coming-of-age voyage. I stared at the pool of liquid at the bottom of the bottle, dazzled by its luminous effervescence and haunted by ambiguous memories. I tipped the bottle and let the spectacle of liquid and light cascade up and down the sides of the glass. I uncorked the bottle, brought it to my nose, and smelled its contents. I was no longer the inexperienced, ignorant youth who had first encountered the liquid years ago. Nevertheless, I still could not identify the fragrance that escaped from the open bottle.

I closed my eyes and savoured the exotic aroma. My lips caressed the mouth of the bottle as I recalled—with both wonder and unease—how I had come to possess it. The dampness on the glass ridge shocked me. I clamped down on the memories and emotions the taste evoked as firmly as I recorked the bottle. I licked the trace of liquid from my lips.

And I suddenly felt awake and vigorous. And aroused. So aroused, it pushed everything else from my mind. So aroused, it hurt. I decided to take a shower, planning to masturbate while enjoying the hot steam.

As I entered the bathroom, I saw him in the mirror. His beautiful face. The subtle, mesmerizing colours running through his hair.

But he was wearing my clothes, was standing where I stood.

I had turned into a doppelganger of the mysterious lover who had left only that bottle behind—exactly as he'd looked all those years ago, when he'd kissed me.

I collapsed, tears storming out of me. Then my head exploded, and the bathroom vanished around me, to be replaced by—

I am a boy looking at myself everywhere in the world. I am everyBODY in the world. I gorge on my own flesh, my arm stuffed down my throat. HE is nowhere. I am dancing. There are many of me. I am a boy. I am a girl. I am a man. I am a woman. I am dancing. With each whirl I take off a piece of clothing. The boys, the girls, the men, the women—I, I, I, and I take off my clothes. I and I and I and I have sex. I MAN *insert my penis in an anus* BOY *in a mouth* GIRL *in a vagina* WOMAN. *I* WOMAN *rub my vulva on the stomachs of myself* BOYGIRLMAN *lying on the ground. I laugh and cry. I am reading a book. Every page is a mirror. I see myself but I do not look like me. I am handsome. I am beautiful. I am charming. I am elegant. I am strong. I am vulnerable. I am everywhere and it is me. It is my body. I am not me. I am a boy. I look down* MY HEAD TURNS AND SPINS *and there is a boy licking my anus but it is not him. It is not me. He looks up at me. Smiling and laughing, laughing and crying. He kisses me. I taste semen in his mouth. I take off my penis and offer it to him. I run. There are many people. None of them are me. None of them are him. They all laugh but they do not cry. I shout:* WHO ARE YOU? WHY ARE YOU NOT HIM? *Still they do not cry. Where is he? The sound of beating wings. I can see myself* IT IS NOT THE BODY OF A BOY *running, my cloven hooves hitting the pavement, the amber blood coursing through the thick veins bulging from my hairless naked body, the lack of genitals at my crotch, the huge mouth with thick amber lips and big white teeth gaping from my belly, my full breasts covered with thick amber veins bumping against my chest. My head is spinning out of control. I am not him. On the one side, below the ring of eyes crowning my head, a penis and scrotum protrude from my face, flapping around. On the other side, a wet vulva opens deep down inside my throat. I cannot cry. No tears will come. I am not a boy. I hear the furious din of beating wings. I do not see him. The black shapes come and smother me* THE BODY THAT IS NOT A BOY. *There is no sound. Swirling rainbows of* GREENBLUEBROWN *erupt from the darkness. There are bodies everywhere. Of every shape. I recognize no body.*

I woke up with a debilitating headache, having no idea how long I'd slept—if I'd slept at all—profoundly disgusted by my . . . hallucination? . . . nightmare? . . . whatever that had been. I was terrified by its oppressive self-loathing. And what was I to make of the monstrous hermaphroditic creature "I" had turned into? Cold dread spread through my bones.

I had fallen on the floor, and I'd bruised my head

and elbows. Reluctantly, I propped myself back up. The mirror revealed I was myself again. Not a monster, and not my mysterious lover either.

It was that bottle. That strange liquid was some sort of drug that produced powerful hallucinations. Of course—I thought—I had never turned into anything or anyone else.

Ignoring my aches and bruises, I stomped to the shelf where I kept the bottle. I picked it up, considered smashing it. Or just throwing it away. Instead, I put it in a box in the broom closet, unable to deal with it decisively.

I spent the rest of the day dawdling—doing this and that, not really accomplishing anything, distracting myself with little pleasures: listening to favourite records, rereading cherished stories. In the end, it was another long, dreary day. But I managed to dismiss that frightening vision as nothing more than the result of that awful potion combined with my fragile emotional state.

A few days later, I ran into my young blond lover at the university; but her eyes avoided mine, and I had to acknowledge what, I suddenly realized, I already knew. Ah well . . . I had claimed not to want serious attachments, hadn't I? I'd promised her sexual fun and ended up needing emotional comfort.

I broke off all my sexual liaisons and for a year or so mainly kept to myself. I needed that year to redefine my identity, to dig within myself, to discover the tools with which to rebuild myself.

I pushed the bottle—its contents and its disturbing visions—far from my thoughts, relegating it to a neglected corner of my consciousness.

I took to solitude rather well. It reminded me of my childhood, when I spent days sequestered in my bedroom, content with the company of my books.

Eventually, I made new friends, or rather acquaintances. I met no-one significant. I shared lunches, occasionally went out to the theatre and such. I surprised myself by staying celibate. My sex drive had simply faded away. Years passed. I took a position as Associate Professor in my department.

One spring, I flew to my hometown, dreading a family event that I couldn't avoid—a cousin's wedding—and my parents died in a fire. The house burned down—a kitchen accident, the investigators later established. The street was sealed off; my cab had to drop me off a block away. It was an impressive, angry blaze. After it had spent its fury, nothing from the house was salvageable. I was told my parents died quickly. The wedding wasn't postponed. I didn't attend.

Mom and Dad had always been so kind to me. Ours had been a peaceful and supportive household. I didn't have a single resentful memory, and yet I found myself unable to grieve. Not numb, not sad, not even relieved; just—and I hate to admit this—indifferent.

A year later, I used the money from the estate to buy a new house. I was charmed by the building upon first seeing it. The deal was quickly concluded, and within weeks I left my old apartment. I successfully arranged the main floor in a few days, making it fully operational and pleasing to inhabit.

The upstairs of the house remained in complete disarray. I had been renovating, organizing, and unpacking for weeks, but I just couldn't seem to make things gel. I was too excited at the prospect of creating this dream space. I wanted to do everything at once, with the enthusiasm of a teenage boy, but the dwindling energy of a man nearing forty. The box now before me had not been opened in years, judging by the brittleness of the packing tape. A box my mother had packed many years ago when I had left my parents' home for university. Despite the mess around me, the pull of curiosity and nostalgia overwhelmed other concerns, and I tore open the box with an eagerness I hadn't felt in years, maybe decades.

It was filled with semi-forgotten books—all books I'd purchased at Lost Pages. They had such sensationalistic titles: *The Transfiguration of Gilgamesh*, *Antediluvian Folktales*, *Intrigues and Scandals of the Lemurian Court*, *The Trickster among Us*, *Great Migrations of Extinct Branches of the Genus Homo*, and so forth. Just the kind of thing to excite a lonely boy's imagination. The more scholarly titles on the shelves of Lost Pages, many of which featured names and words—not to mention languages—that were, to me, alien and unrecognizable, had always intimidated me, though the serious young boy I had been would never have admitted it.

Antediluvian Folktales exerted a particular pull on me. Why had I never unpacked these before? They'd lain forgotten for so long. I grabbed the folktale collection, and the shop's distinctive green, blue, and brown bookmark fell out. Ignoring the huge task before me, I opened the book and started reading. After the first half-dozen short tales, I started remembering when I'd first read the book at age fourteen, in late August, just before school started. And then an image lodged itself in my mind, from a story I now remembered for the first time since then. I flipped through the book impatiently, trying to find a particular passage to confirm my memory. On my fifth or sixth run-through, I found it: ". . . the rich fullness of his wings, the shifting colours of his feathers, the bright sparkle of his scales, the sharpness of his beak . . ." My heart beat anxiously against my chest. I had to take several deep breaths to calm myself. I flipped back to the beginning of the tale, "Why We Dream Nightmares."

Long ago, in the time before the Earth had taken the shape of a globe and so night was night and day was day throughout the world, the Shifpan-Shap flew every night, battling nightmares with their mighty weapons. After the sun disappeared over the horizon, the nightmares covered the whole sky with their great number, determined to descend into the dreams of women, men, children, and animals. Every night, the Shifpan-Shap fought them to a standstill, never letting a single nightmare break through their ranks. If only one of them entered the realm of dreams, the war would be lost, and nightmares would plague the land of dreams forevermore. In those days, the night sky was pitch black; no stars could shine through the dense darkness of the attacking horde. When the morning sun rose on the horizon, the nightmares cowered back into the dark embrace of their creator, Yamesh-Lot, who yearned to rule the land of dreams.

Every morning, the Shifpan-Shap uttered a great cry of victory, mocking the retreating nightmares and rousing humanity and other animals to wakefulness. The Shifpan-Shap then flew back into the city of Shifpan-Ur— the lustre of their green, blue, and brown feathers revealed by the morning sun—to rest and prepare for the next night's campaign.

One of the Shifpan-Shap, Behl Jezath, was a proud and fierce warrior. Many of the Shifpan-Shap admired his youthful beauty, and the delights of his body were much coveted. Although Behl Jezath knew the love of many, he had only love for himself. Often he would hover over still water to glance at his reflection. How he admired the rich fullness of his wings, the shifting colours of his feathers, the bright sparkle of his scales, the sharpness of his beak, the smooth girth of his phallus!

Behl Jezath grew older, as all Shifpan-Shap did in those days. His wings thinned out, his scales lost some of their sheen, his beak acquired a certain bluntness, and wrinkles appeared on his phallus. Before, his splendid beauty had been so dazzling that it outshone his great vanity. Now that his beauty was dimming, the harsh glare of his pride drove his lovers away.

Embittered, the aging Shifpan-Sho spent more and more time away from his people. In broad daylight, he flew far from Shifpan-Ur. From high above he spied on the women, men, and children that the Green Blue and Brown God had entrusted to the Shifpan-Shap's protection. The lustful eyes of Behl Jezath fell on the young men just old enough to no longer be called boys. He saw them play with their burgeoning genitals, enjoying themselves and each other.

The Green Blue and Brown God had forbidden the Shifpan-Shap from fornicating with mortal animals, upon punishment of having their wings torn from their backs, but Behl Jezath's lust was overpowering. Day after day he flew high in the sky spying on the young men, desiring their muscular bodies and their smooth phalluses, tempting himself with this forbidden passion.

One day, Behl Jezath decided to hide behind some trees, near a spot where the young men often gathered for their sex games. He wanted to be close to the young men. He wanted to be able to smell their muskiness and to see their beautiful bodies up close.

The young men came as expected, and the hidden Shifpan-Sho smelled their young manliness and admired their muscular bodies. Their proximity was intoxicating to the old warrior. Behl Jezath took his wrinkled phallus in the palm of his claw and rubbed himself to ejaculation. So intense was his pleasure that his wings unfurled in splendid glory. He uttered a great shrill cry. The young men scattered in fear.

Behl Jezath flew away, back to Shifpan-Ur to rest in preparation for that night's battle with the nightmare legions of Yamesh-Lot.

And, as he had been doing with increasing frequency, he dreamed of the young men and the sex games he yearned to play with them.

That night, a nightmare embroiled in close combat with Behl Jezath smelled the lingering aroma of his dreams. The nightmare whispered into Behl Jezath's ear and said to the Shifpan-Sho: "Warrior! My master, Yamesh-Lot, can make your dreams come true. Let me go to him now and let us meet again tomorrow night in this very spot. I will bring you the means to fulfill your dreams."

The lust coursing through Behl Jezath's veins was very powerful, and he let the nightmare return to its dark master.

The sun rose. The nightmares retreated. The Shifpan-Shap uttered their cry of triumph and returned to Shifpan-Ur to rest in preparation for the next night's battle.

Behl Jezath could not sleep all day, restless with conflicting impulses and emotions: anticipation, lust, pride, honour, loyalty, betrayal, shame.

The following night, the nightmare returned as promised, clutching a bottle. The
creature whispered in the old warrior's ear:
"Let me pass, and you can take this bottle,
the cornucopia of ambrosia. This drink will
transform you into your heart's desire. One
sip, and you can disguise yourself as a young
human male—or whatever you desire—veiled
from the wrath of the Green Blue and Brown
God and free to enjoy the bodies of young
men. As long as one drop remains, it will
forever replenish itself. This bottle is Yamesh-
Lot's gift to you, warrior, if you let me pass and
enter the realm of mortal dreams."

Behl Jezath replied: "How do I know this
is not a trick, nightmare? You could easily be
lying in order to win the war for your dark
master."

The nightmare immediately answered: "Warrior, I propose a test! Form a clear picture in
your mind of your heart's desire, and I will let a
drop of the ambrosia fall on your tongue. One
drop will transform you only for a short time,

but it will be enough for you to believe in the power of this beverage."

Behl Jezath agreed to this test. In his mind's eye, he saw himself as a young Shifpan-Sho with his wings rich and dense, his scales bright as little suns, his phallus smooth and large, for that was his true desire.

The nightmare let a drop fall on the tongue of the aging Behl Jezath. The Shifpan-Sho felt his wings fill out, he could see his scales glitter even in the darkness of night, and his phallus was restored to its full girth.

He remembered the smell of the young men and his newly young body was filled with lust for them. Then, the effect of the one drop of ambrosia wore off, and the body of Behl Jezath regained its true age.

The nightmare said: "Warrior, that was the effect of only one drop! Are you convinced? Are we agreed?"

Behl Jezath hesitated, but only for a moment. "Yes," he said. "Yes, we are agreed, nightmare."

The next day, the Green Blue and Brown God was furious with the Shifpan-Shap for letting a nightmare into the land of dreams. He punished them by turning them all into immortal skeletons, forever denied all sensual pleasures. When the Green Blue and Brown God meted out his punishment, Behl Jezath was hidden from the god's view. Thanks to the properties of the nightmare's bribe, he was disguised as a young man, trying to find other young men with whom to play sex games. However, the young men no longer played sex games amongst themselves. Their new nightmares taught them to fear such things. Frustrated, Behl Jezath flew back to Shifpan-Ur. His punished brethren saw his unspoiled form. They knew then that he had betrayed them to Yamesh-Lot, and they banished him from their midst for all time.

And so it came to pass that Yamesh-Lot won the war over the land of dreams. However, his nightmares no longer covered the night sky, and the shining stars were the source of new dreams for humanity, dreams outside the reach of the dark lord.

Trembling slightly, I sat on the floor, silently but nervously pondering this story. After awhile, I calmed down again and read the rest of the collection. There were no other references to these characters, to this tale. In an appendix, the author quoted some sources and suggested further reading for each story. "Why We Dream Nightmares" had but one reference: *Ambrosia: The History of a Cornucopia of Transformation.*

I picked up the bookmark from the floor, remembering the many hours spent at Lost Pages. I knew I would not find the volume anywhere else. The book was on the shelves of the shop, waiting for me. It had to be.

It would have to wait, I thought. The next few days were filled with engagements from which I could not, in good conscience, extricate myself. I was also dimly aware of, although not dealing with, the anxieties that gnawed at me: about where all this might lead and the possibility that it would, in fact, lead to nowhere. Almost any excuse was good enough to cause a delay. I suppose I could have called the bookshop in advance to make sure they had the book, or to ask to have it put aside for me, or to ask to have it delivered to me. But I needed the quest, the adventure of visiting the place once again, of finding the book myself.

I knew in which box to find the bottle. I took it out and held it up to my face. The pool of liquid was now several centimetres deep, the bottle nearly half full.

Three days later, tense and anxious, I was on a plane to my hometown. The last time I'd been there was to settle the last of my parents' affairs, about eight months ago.

As I had hoped, I found the book at Lost Pages.

Inside the bookshop, I recognized the young boy who had once been the shopkeeper's assistant, now grown up. He appeared now to be running the place with an assistant of his own, a girl in her early teens. I did not attempt to identify myself to him as a long-lost customer. I quickly made my purchase, promising myself to return one day and take the time to enjoy the experience. This short trip was an indulgence my schedule could barely accommodate.

I took a cab to the airport. The terminal was bustling. Long lineups writhed in irritated impatience. Indecipherable announcements fizzled from unseen speakers. Travellers and personnel crisscrossed the huge room every which way.

A hand brushed against mine. I was aroused by the intensity of that elusive touch. I looked around, in vain, hoping to find the source of this furtive sexual thrill. I shivered—like an eager teenage boy.

Frustrated, I joined the lineup for my airline and eventually secured a boarding pass. My plane was scheduled to start boarding in fifty minutes. I settled on a bench and savoured the anticipation of cracking open my new acquisition, eager to find answers to questions I'd long neglected.

About ten minutes later, I suddenly felt very dizzy, as if all the blood had rushed out of my head. I had to brace myself on my neighbour. At the contact, he turned his head toward me.

His face was beautiful. He now appeared to be about my age, but how could I not recognize the features of the boy who had been the first to kiss me? His greying hair had lost some of it lustre, but I thought I could still glimpse hints of green, blue, and brown.

Staring at the bulge in my pants, he laughed. With the embarrassment of a boy, I noticed my conspicuously large erection.

I regained my composure—partly because of the pleasant nostalgia his good humour called up, but also because I recognized the comical nature of my situation. I chuckled, but then a spiky chill tore down my chest.

I knew who he was, now. What he was.

I opened my mouth, ready to . . . interrogate him? Plead with him? Or . . . I never found out what I would have said. He placed two fingers on my mouth, tenderly silencing me. He looked hurt. No. Something else. Some emotion I couldn't grasp. I longed to know him better, to understand his every gesture, his every expression.

He seemed to shrug off whatever he was

feeling, and he smiled. He gave me a look—of deep compassion, perhaps? It made me feel profoundly lonely.

I realized then how, these past few years, I still hadn't learned to care about anyone. I still protected myself against intimacy. Now, I was overcome by how much I wanted to care about him, care for him. It suddenly seemed so obvious to me that I'd spent all these years trying to recapture the transcendence I'd experienced when he'd seduced me and, failing to ever again reach those heights of ecstasy, how I'd shielded myself against my inevitable disappointments.

He clamped his hand behind my neck and gave me a fierce kiss. He released me, and nodded upward, silently telling me that I should go. My flight was being called.

I looked into his eyes, but they refused to yield any answers. Stifling tears, I nodded back, got up, and walked toward the gate. I didn't look back. I was afraid to see in his eyes the gaze of a stranger. The sound of beating wings drowned out the ambient noise around me. Did I imagine that?

I told myself that it was his wish that I leave.

Two days later, in my house, in this upstairs room that was still not organized to my satisfaction, I sat with my eyes shut; the book, *Ambrosia: The History of a Cornucopia of Transformation*, closed on my lap. I studiously read every word. How had the author found all that information? I felt a surge of envy at his ability to uncover so much about my seducer's mysterious life.

The book revealed many of the identities Behl Jezath adopted and speculated on many more. It detailed years, centuries, millennia spent in solitude—hiding and fleeing from the pride of his youth and its consequences. It told of epochs wiped from human memory. It described how Behl Jezath's continued life depended on the bottle of ambrosia, the memento of his terrible moment of weakness.

What would happen to him now? Why did he give me the bottle? Why had I been such a coward at the airport? Too many unanswerable questions. . . .

I stared at the bottle. It rested on the side table next to my armchair. The light from the window caught the slowly rising pool of ambrosia. Rainbows danced and swirled, flowing and erupting from the amber fluid.

That night, I sat on the roof and tried to look at the stars. But it was overcast. I closed my eyes, felt the chill of the early autumn wind against my cheeks, and dreamt of the furious beating of multicoloured wings.

When Lucas called out to her as he knocked on her door, Aydee realized that she was crying, and had been doing so for a while.

"Are you okay, Aydee? You've been cooped up in there for hours. Dinner's ready, if you're hungry."

She hesitated before replying, worried her voice might betray her tears. "I'm fine. I just have a lot of thinking to do today. You don't have to worry about me."

"You know I always will, though. Come down whenever you're hungry. I'll leave the leftovers in the fridge, top shelf. But take whatever time you need."

A dog scratched at the door to be let in. Lucas asked, "Can Gold come in?"

"Sure."

Lucas opened the door just enough for Gold to barrel in—Aydee noticed how Lucas was careful not to peek inside uninvited—and then shut it again. Lucas trusted her so much.

She never showed him the letter.

CHAPTER 4

Dark Tendrils

Kurt was four years old when he found the rock shaped like a star. His grandparents lived next to a little beach. He spent that whole summer there, loving every moment of it. They built fires, waded in the ocean, hunted for seashells. For many years, even into adulthood, whenever he held the star-stone and closed his eyes, he would smell the ocean the way it had smelled to him then: like another world. Like the promise of magic. If such a majestic thing as the ocean were possible—if the world contained such an immense creation, and if that creation's fragrance could be so intoxicatingly complex—then anything could be possible.

One morning, shortly after the break of dawn, while the rest of the family was still asleep, he had walked toward that vast expanse of water, eyes closed, letting the smell transport him beyond anything he'd ever imagined. Then he stepped on something that scraped his foot.

Startled, he opened his eyes and bent down to investigate. Half-buried in the sand was a lopsided, five-pointed star—a speckled rock, just a bit bigger than his four-year-old hand, sculpted into that shape by time and water.

He saw in that rock a mysterious, seductive beauty. He was convinced that his discovery heralded the promise of a wondrous future.

He kept it. He kept it for years.

Why had Kurt insisted that he and Holly go to that party at Carol's? He'd forgotten why, but he wished they had stayed in—had sex, watched TV, played cards, whatever.

Carol's spacious apartment overflowed with guests. The effect, oddly, was to make it seem even bigger, like endless catacombs invaded and overrun by a throng of decadent bacchants. Kurt knew about half the people there: a good mix of familiar faces and new people, exactly how he liked parties. Beer flowed. Joints passed from hand to hand. Smoke was blown from mouth to mouth. Flirtation was mandatory. At first, he'd been having a great time.

Then he noticed Holly chatting with Giovanni. At the sight of him he'd felt something slither down his back.

He didn't think that Holly knew him. Certainly, he'd never mentioned him to her. He realized then that he should have—a long time ago, to warn her. But shame had proved stronger than caution. Kurt had met Giovanni about five years previously but it had been four years since they'd last seen each other.

Even from across the room, Kurt could spot the cruelty in his dark eyes. Giovanni had the blackest eyes, like gateways into something best left undiscovered. His face always seemed to be on the verge of a sneer. Once, Kurt had been attracted to that darkness, that condescending arrogance.

Kurt knew from friends that Giovanni still occasionally stepped inside the periphery of his social circle. It was inevitable that they would eventually cross paths again. Mark, Tony, and Jessica occasionally gushed over him, saying how charming he was. But they hadn't known him back then; they weren't from that old crowd—and those people Kurt had lost touch with. Whenever anyone brought Giovanni up in conversation, Kurt found a way to change the subject.

Giovanni had been older than any of Kurt's friends back then and was older than anyone at the party that night. Late thirties at least, though it was hard to tell how old exactly; sometimes he seemed much older. Kurt used to ask him about his age, but Giovanni had never given him a straight answer.

Kurt saw Giovanni place his fingers on Holly's bare shoulder. Kurt grew hot with rage. He wanted to grab Holly and leave the party. Get her as far from Giovanni as possible. But, no matter how hard he tried, he couldn't get near them, as if the crowd were conspiring to keep them apart. He tried to shout at Holly, but his voice was thin, raspy, muffled. The whole party became hazy, dreamlike, nightmarish.

Kurt had a high tolerance for alcohol—usually. He didn't tend to get drunk, just jolly. That night, though, his joviality turned into mean drunkenness. He argued with everyone around him. Not making any sense. Being a jerk. The party had completely lost its glitter, becoming a blur of oozing anger.

The next thing Kurt knew, it was dawn, and he and Holly were walking home, shouting, fighting.

In their two years together, they had never quarrelled. Ever. On the rare occasions when a potential conflict presented itself, they'd always known how to talk things through calmly. He loved that about them, their relationship.

Kurt didn't even really know what they were fighting about. Holly was questioning him about some teenager—a dark-skinned girl with long, multicoloured braids—he'd apparently been chatting up.

"She kept pointing at me. Whispering in your ear."

"I can't remember. I was drunk."

"I saw her slip you a piece of paper. Her phone number?"

"I said, I was drunk—I don't remember her. I don't remember anything." But Kurt fumbled through his pockets anyway. He found something: a bookmark. Holly leaned in to see, but Kurt pushed her away.

Lost Pages it read, in bold blue letters on a brown background, with the address in small green type. *Whatever*, he thought, shoving it back into his pocket.

From that moment on they fought about everything and nothing. Every day. About the most inane things. Too quickly, arguing became their predominant mode of communication.

One evening, after five weeks of this torment, Holly stormed out after yet another screaming match. Something about the volume of the TV while they were watching the news. Stupid. Inconsequential.

Near midnight, she finally came home, with Giovanni in tow.

Giovanni, again. I should have guessed, Kurt thought.

Holly didn't say a word to Kurt. She walked right past him, without acknowledging him in any way. Giovanni greeted Kurt with a "Hello" whose a tone left him feeling exposed and vulnerable.

Then they started making out right in front of Kurt. On the couch. Taking off each other's clothes. Fondling each other. As if Kurt weren't there. Or maybe especially because he was there.

Kurt didn't know how to react. He just stood there silently, stunned into numbness.

Holly continued to ignore him. But Giovanni kept stealing these cold glances at him.

At this stage, anger was pointless. The sight of them—the girl he loved giving herself to a man he despised and feared, to a man who reminded him of his own weakness, stupidity, and shame—filled him with hatred and self-loathing, but he felt compelled to watch.

When they positioned themselves in a sixty-nine,

Kurt had finally had enough. He shut himself in the bedroom, closing the door quietly. He went to bed without bothering to take his clothes off.

Kurt thought about leaving the apartment, but, as painful as it was, staying also afforded him a measure of control; it allowed him to focus on the transgressions that were occurring in his presence rather than letting his imagination run wildly paranoid with much worse horrors. Holly and Giovanni went at it for hours, groaning and moaning and screaming.

Despite that, Kurt eventually settled into an unrestful doze.

When Kurt saw the first hint of dawn through the window, he decided to get up and go out. Have breakfast at The Small Easy. Try to get his head straight. Figure out what to do.

But he couldn't budge.

Frustrated at being unable to get out of bed, he tried to move specific parts of his body, but he couldn't even wiggle his fingers. His entire body was cocooned inside some kind of force field. It stung, producing a mild electric current every time he tried to move. The field pulled itself tighter against him, crushing his chest. He panicked, uselessly.

Kurt felt a presence—not so much with him, but directed at him. He could move his eyes, though not his head. He glanced around, but there was nobody. The bedroom seemed undisturbed. It struck him that he couldn't hear anything—no noise leaking in from other apartments, no sounds from the city outside. Even this early in the morning there was always some kind of background din. The absolute silence—deafness?—made him feel intensely isolated, more than he would have ever guessed. The helplessness of being trapped in his bed combined with that sense of utter isolation from the world—it terrified him.

The pressure of the cocoon around him increased. His lungs were being squeezed; he could barely breathe.

He willed every part of his body to move. His terror gave way to rage, and he finally managed to open his mouth. Kurt focused all his energy on screaming. Although he sensed the beginnings of the scream in his throat and felt it move through his mouth, the scream hit the invisible cocoon and bounced back into his throat, choking him, without making the slightest sound.

Kurt intensified his efforts to break free, but he only succeeded in slightly budging his head. Some feeling of dread compelled him to look at the door; as he did, it opened slowly. Holly walked in, leaving the door open. She was naked, her short hair suddenly grown to shoulder length, her normally hazel irises a deep, unnatural black.

The cocoon crackled all around Kurt, squeezing him ever tighter, so tight that his rib cage contracted under the pressure.

Holly pulled the covers off him. She was smiling ghoulishly. Without a word, she unzipped him and worked on his cock with her hands. Kurt's erection was hard enough to hurt him. He tried to shout at her to stop, but the cocoon allowed not even a whimper to escape.

She sat on top of Kurt and rode his erection, her black eyes laughing at him.

Helpless, he felt the semen begin to build and rise, but he didn't want to come. Not like this.

Then, just as he thought he could no longer hold himself back, his consciousness was ripped out of his body. His incorporeal self rose rapidly toward the ceiling. A malevolent presence radiated from beyond that threshold, pulling him toward it. He resisted with all the strength his terror afforded him. He knew with utter certainty that he would not survive the crossing.

Below, the demonic Holly was still riding his cock, writhing in ecstasy on his inert body.

Kurt's sense of time split in two: he experienced himself rushing toward the ceiling at tremendous speed, yet every second felt like hours. His fear increased with every passing moment, the malevolence ever more tangible. Calling to him. Wanting him. And just when he thought he could no longer resist—

—he landed in his body, screaming.

Of Holly, there was no sign. Kurt was fully dressed. The sheet still covered him. And the door was closed, as if he'd hallucinated everything. Or dreamt it. But he knew he hadn't. He still felt the pain on his skin, in his throat, in his lungs.

Holly—wearing a tattered white T-shirt, her hair restored to its normal length, her eyes their natural hazel—ran into the bedroom, calling Kurt's name with frightened concern. She'd never heard him scream before. She took his hand, caressed his chest. "Oh baby, I'm so sorry," she said. "He's gone now. For good. Please. I went crazy. That wasn't me. You know it wasn't."

Kurt didn't want to contemplate life without Holly, even after all this. He knew she wasn't to blame. He knew what Giovanni was capable of. There was nothing to forgive.

Kurt told her what had just happened: the strange paralysis, her demonic doppelganger—all of it.

Holly held him silently for a few minutes, her hands under his shirt, against his bare skin. Her nails dug into the flesh of his back, and he felt closer to her than he had in weeks.

Then, she said, "I need to tell you something. You're not going to like this." Kurt didn't have the strength to hear this, whatever it was. But Holly barrelled on regardless. "He kept asking about you, but I wouldn't say anything. He said there was something you always kept hidden from him. Something that you'd invested with a part of yourself. Something that gave you the will to resist. But he never could figure out what. My eyes must have betrayed me—betrayed you—because he saw it. The star. On the mantle in the living room. And then . . . I don't know why . . . but I told him the story. Your story."

"Oh fuck, Holly. . . ."

"I'm sorry. I'm so sorry. He took it. He stole it. He just laughed. I couldn't stop him. I couldn't even yell to warn you. I don't know why. I just couldn't. Something about those black eyes. . . ."

It would have been so easy for Kurt to lash out at Holly, then, to make her pay because he felt betrayed. He was tempted to give in to that, but what was the point? Kurt had let this happen. It was his fault Giovanni was in their lives at all.

Holly said, "Let's get it back now. I think I know where he went." She avoided Kurt's eyes when she revealed that, and paused awkwardly before continuing. "We can't let him get away with all this."

"Holly, let's not. Let's just forget him. Let's just not ever see him again. Either of us. Promise me you'll never go anywhere near him again."

"I promise, baby."

Kurt nodded and clasped her hand. "Besides, the star would only remind me of Giovanni, now. Its magic is ruined. Corrupted."

Holly asked, "Okay, but . . . How do you know him? Why does he have it in for you? Why are you so scared?"

Back then, Kurt had always held back; Giovanni had pestered him about it. As much as the older man had fascinated Kurt for awhile, some instinct toward self-preservation had made him resist the urge to fully open up.

Since spotting Giovanni at Carol's party, Kurt had been trying to avoid his memories, even more than he usually did. But now he had an urgent need to trust Holly, to stop hiding from her. So he finally told her about his time with Giovanni.

"Back in university, a bunch of us got interested in dreams. Every Saturday night we'd fuel up on beer and pot and tell each other our best and weirdest dreams of the week. This girl, Bethany, got really into it, more so than any of us, and one night she brought this creepy old guy with her. Giovanni. At first, a bunch of us snickered at the sight of him. He looked like some kind of perv. But Bethany was clearly impressed with him. He was an expert, she told us. He could tell us what our dreams meant. He charmed us, somehow telling each of us what we most wanted to hear. Were we that transparent?"

Kurt paused. Holly waited, didn't rush him. She squeezed his hand tighter.

"Soon, we began meeting every evening. Increasingly everyone's dreams took on a darkly erotic aspect, and that spilled over into the meetings. It was getting too creepy for me, but all the others seemed so into it. I didn't want to be, you know, the square. Giovanni would usually spend the night with one or more of us. I don't know that he even had a place of his own."

Holly interrupted, "He does, now."

That brought images of the two of them together

to Kurt's mind. Kurt must have let his revulsion show; Holly cringed and looked away.

Kurt remembered Giovanni in his own bed, fondling him, cajoling him into revealing his most intimate secrets.

"Then Bethany died in her sleep, and it all changed for me. Giovanni was with her that night. I was convinced that he was responsible. Regardless, there was no evidence of foul play, and her death was attributed to 'natural causes.' But the spell was broken, for me at least. Maybe for a few of the others, but I'm not sure. I was the first to leave the group, and I broke off contact with everyone. That's the last time I'd seen him before that night at Carol's. I never wanted to think about him again."

Kurt wondered if one day he and Holly would ever be ready to discuss what she went through while she was in Giovanni's thrall. He wasn't ready to hear it. She said, "Let's forget about him. Let's concentrate on the future. Our future."

Kurt enfolded Holly in his arms, pressed her against his chest as hard as he could, wanting more than anything to trust Holly again.

Kurt and Holly resumed their lives as best they could. Things between them never returned to exactly what they'd been before; that had been lost forever. Kurt thought, *Something else that creep stole from me. From us.*

They stopped going to parties; it was too vivid a reminder of how Holly had met Giovanni. There was no fun for them there anymore. Their social life suffered for it; some friends dropped out of their lives, but not all of them. They became much more domestic. There was pleasure in that, too.

Kurt liked to think they were building a new life, that they had faith in each other. It was awkward sometimes, but Kurt was confident that they both wanted to be together. Yet sometimes he caught himself doubting: maybe that was only how he wanted things to be; nevertheless, he let himself believe that. Ignoring the evidence; ignoring his gnawing anxieties.

Holly never mentioned Giovanni, or her time with him. It was a wound neither of them seemed eager to reopen, though sometimes that silence weighed heavily.

Sometimes, she would start to say something to Kurt, and then stop herself after a word or two. Every time that happened he quietly feared that the aborted subject was Giovanni, and he was selfishly grateful for her silence.

Kurt occasionally suffered through snippets of that strange dream—various permutations of paralysis, demonic visitation, and out-of-body experience. He was always a bit shaken the morning after, but he told himself they were only nightmares; he ignored them as much as possible.

Then, the nightmare struck every night for an entire week. Each night, the sensation that his life was in danger increased.

It was still the dead of night when he emerged from the paralysis for the seventh consecutive time. His whole body was drenched in cold sweat. He was too freaked out, too frightened, to go back to sleep. He slipped out of bed, careful not to wake Holly. He needed to move around, to get some air. He dressed and went out for a walk.

Outside, it was chillier than he'd expected. He

dug his hands into his jacket pockets and scraped a finger against something. He pulled it out. It was that bookmark from Carol's party: *Lost Pages*. He read the address; it was at least an hour's walk from where he was. *What the hell*, he thought. He might as well have a destination, even if the bookstore would be closed at that time of night. He needed to occupy his mind.

The shop's sign was as garish as its bookmark, with gaudy mismatched colours and cheesy, ornate font. There was some light inside, so he peeked through the window. There was a guy sitting at the counter. Kurt went in.

The tiny store was crammed full with books ... and dogs. At least half a dozen, of all sizes. Kurt couldn't stand being in there. The smell of dust and dogs. The cramped messiness. *Who would ever want to spend any time in this dump?* He nodded an apologetic smile at the big, tall guy at the cash and turned to leave. But something on the top shelf of a bookcase next to the door caught his eye before he'd made it outside: a leatherbound tome with a faded painting of

Giovanni's face on the front cover. The book looked very old. Too old.

Kurt grabbed it; but the words inside were in a language he couldn't read. He couldn't even recognize the alphabet. It was like nothing he'd ever seen.

"What is this?" Kurt shouted to the bookseller, waving the book in his face.

The bookseller stayed calm. He asked Kurt, "You know that man on the cover?"

Kurt glared at him, unable to speak, not knowing what to say. One of the dogs sniffed him; Kurt glared at it, too, and it left him alone.

"You're in serious danger," the bearish man warned Kurt. "He worships Yamesh-Lot, the lord of nightmares. He collects sacrifices for his god."

"Nightmares? Sacrifices?"

The man looked into Kurt's eyes, considered what he saw. "Aqtuqsi," he said.

"What?" Kurt couldn't wrap his tongue around the unfamiliar syllables.

The man called out, "Aydee," and a teenage girl

with creamy brown skin and long, multicoloured braids emerged from the back of the store. "Can you get me that book on aqtuqsi?" She quickly zeroed in on the book in question, as if she knew the location of every speck of dust in that chaotic mess. The bookseller nodded toward Kurt, and she handed him the book.

The book was a tiny hardback with dark blue cardboard covers. On the front was a brown-coloured relief of a sleeping man enveloped in a radiating glow. In blue, the word "Aqtuqsi" was printed below the illustration.

The girl said, "About time you came by."

For the first time, Kurt remembered her. From the party: touching his wrist; whispering Giovanni's name into his ear.

The bookseller said, "We can help you."

What the fuck?

Still holding both books, Kurt ran outside before either of them could say anything else. His heart pounded in his chest. Sweat ran down his face. He thought, *Those people. They were screwing with me.*

How do they know about me? Giovanni. This has to be part of Giovanni's game, whatever that is. Yamesh-Lot? What nonsense. How gullible do they think I am?

Kurt stopped running and caught his breath. He oriented himself and headed over to The Small Easy, his favourite 24-hour joint. He downed his first cup of hot coffee like it was water.

Sipping his refill, he examined the book with Giovanni's face on the cover; it really was entirely written in some weird, unfamiliar language. Kurt turned to the other book. This was it: the explanation for what had been plaguing him. *Aqtuqsi*, an Inuktitut word that translated roughly as "my nightmare": a supernatural attack by a spirit or sorcerer that paralyzed the body by preying on the mind when it was at its weakest. The phenomenon was known in other cultures under various names— the Chinese called it *gui ya*, ghost oppression; for the Japanese, it was *kanashibari*; in the West Indies, the term was *kokma*; people in Newfoundland named it *old hag*, because the most common variant there involved hallucinating that an old witch was sitting on your chest; even science had a name for it: sleep paralysis—but, this book said, only Inuit shamans had developed defenses against it.

Kurt read that sorcerers, if they held an object that once belonged to you (the stronger the emotional bond to the object, the better), could weave a spell that would constantly gnaw on your mind, thus making you more vulnerable to aqtuqsi. The different chapters included testimonies; a history; a taxonomy of different kinds of aqtuqsi, cataloguing their level of threat or danger; ways to protect yourself; and explanations about the power beyond the threshold. It was all in the book. Everything that had been happening to him, explained. Except *why*—if only he could decipher the other book, the one about Giovanni. That was the real key.

Drinking his third cup of coffee, Kurt caught himself almost drowsing, but he shook his head, willing himself to stay awake. When he looked up, Giovanni was sitting at his table, across from him, snickering. Without thinking, Kurt threw a punch at him. As soon as his fist reached Giovanni's face, his image vanished, and there was nothing left behind. Hitting emptiness upset Kurt's balance. He fell from the chair, his chest hitting the edge of the table. The table rocked, and the mug crashed to the floor, scattering shards of china all over the floor and splattering coffee everywhere.

Sprawled on his back, Kurt shut his eyes for only a second. And opened them to a nightmare.

Everyone in the café had been transformed into demonic creatures so dark that they seemed to consume the light around them. They converged on Kurt, but, as in his nightmares, he was paralyzed, unable even to scream.

Their hands penetrated Kurt's flesh, and he felt his innards and his veins being sucked dry. The more he was drained, the lighter he felt. Suddenly, his immaterial self shot up toward the ceiling while the dark monsters continued to feed on his body. As he was about to collide with the ceiling, or perhaps pass through it, Kurt emerged screaming from the aqtuqsi to find himself lying on the floor of The Small Easy.

The waitress stood over him, asking him questions, but he couldn't concentrate on what she was saying. Patrons were staring at him, their arms sternly crossed across their chests.

Kurt shouted, "Where are my books? The two books I came in with?" He shot to his feet, knocked people aside, searching frantically through the café.

He couldn't find the books.

Hands clutched at him, trying to restrain him. He shouted, "I have to find those books." Tears of rage and desperation ran down his face. The books were nowhere. He struggled free and ran outside.

He ran all the way back to Lost Pages. To confront those people? To ask for help? He didn't know; he couldn't think.

But the store wasn't there anymore. In its place was a laundromat. Kurt was sure that he was on the right street, at the right address. He was certain. He dug through his pockets, but he couldn't find the bookmark anymore.

Tired and confused, Kurt walked back home. Holly had already left for work. Kurt was too weirded out, too terrified, to go to work or to call Holly or to do anything besides drink coffee. And more coffee. Anything to stay awake. Going to sleep would make him too vulnerable.

It was late when Holly finally came home. She took one look at Kurt and immediately acted concerned. Kurt felt too addled to continue facing this on his own. He told her about the recent rash of nightmares, Lost Pages, aqtuqsi, Yamesh-Lot, the books, finding the girl from the party, Giovanni's attack, the bookshop's disappearance—everything.

She listened, but she grew distracted, almost as if Kurt were relaying information she already knew. As he related his story, Kurt's paranoia kept increasing, especially in regards to Holly. When Kurt finished his story, he couldn't even look at Holly anymore. They sat awkwardly, in silence, like strangers.

She broke the silence. "I've been plagued by a recurring nightmare, too. It's not exactly like yours, though."

Kurt didn't look at her while she spoke. He knew he would only sneer. He didn't believe her. He realized he hadn't believed her for a long time. Since Giovanni had come between them.

She continued, "I didn't want to tell you. You seemed to be having such a hard time. I didn't want to make things worse between us by saying anything that might evoke Giovanni or what he'd done to us."

As if Giovanni's shadow weren't always there, a dark impenetrable barrier that forever kept them apart. As if her mere presence weren't reminder enough.

Holly recited her dream: "My dreams are haunted by a god of pure darkness. It doesn't matter what I dream about—childhood, sex, weird adventures, eating—at some point, the god manifests itself. The god is infinitely huge and yet standing right next to me. Dark tendrils shoot out of it and penetrate my body. The god feeds on me, drains me, while I go about my dream. I thought it was just a bad nightmare, some leftover from my guilt about Giovanni, my fear of him." At first, Holly's tone was blank, as if she were remembering lines rather than something she had experienced, but gradually a note of dread crept into her voice. "But now I realize it's something more. Something more ominous. What that bookstore guy said about sacrifices . . . that's what my nightmares feel like. Like I'm being offered to that thing, that god."

Kurt didn't know how to react. He wanted to protect Holly. For a moment, he loved her again, as deeply as he used to. He wanted to, needed to trust Holly, to feel closer to her for having opened up to him. But then the suspicion that it was all a lie, that she was still Giovanni's pawn, resurfaced.

She said, "Let's get this over with. I know where Giovanni lives. Let's confront him and tell him we're not afraid of his tricks anymore."

With that call to action, all of a sudden, Kurt's doubts vanished. He admired Holly, her courage to face up to Giovanni, when he'd only ever been a passive coward. Kurt didn't feel as brave as she did, but he yearned to be swept up in the wake of her courage. "You're right," he said. "We should have done that in the first place. He's just a little creep. A coward who hides behind all this magic mumbo-jumbo."

Giovanni was at the heart of too much darkness in Kurt's past. The idea of confronting him made Kurt queasy, but passively letting Giovanni terrorize him was worse. Both Kurt and Holly had succumbed to him before. But now they were forewarned. And they were together, and stronger for it.

Holly kissed Kurt. Squeezing his hand, her lips brushing his earlobe, she said, "Let's go. Now. Let's make him scared of us for a change."

They fuelled up on coffee. They needed the buzz, the extra adrenaline. Neither of them said what was foremost in Kurt's mind: that they could no longer trust their lives to sleep, that they might never be able to again. And Kurt was utterly exhausted.

They called a cab. They had no plan, but Kurt was determined to push this as far as they had to, uncertain of what, exactly, that could entail.

The cab was waiting for them as they stepped outside. They climbed in the back seat, and Holly called out the address to the driver.

The cab reeked of incense . . . pungent and nauseating. As the car started, Kurt was suddenly overwhelmed with drowsiness. He turned to look at Holly; but it was no longer Holly who sat next to him. His eyes locked with the mocking leer of her demonic doppelganger.

Kurt yelled at the driver to stop, to open the windows. But the cabby ignored him.

The demon Holly murmured Kurt's name in an electrified, distorted voice. Again Kurt screamed at the driver, again with no response. Kurt tried the door, but it was locked and he couldn't get it open.

Kurt struggled to stay awake. As his eyes closed, dark serpentine shapes oozed out of Holly's demonic body and converged on him.

In Kurt's aqtuqsi, he was lying at home, in the bed he shared with Holly. Next to him was Holly's demonic doppelganger. She looked more deformed than in any previous episode, her skin peeling off, her perfectly black eyes glowing menacingly.

Kurt thought: *None of this is real. It can't be.* But it didn't stop him from being terrified.

He tried to break free, to shake himself awake.

But the invisible cocoon sizzled, burning his skin, keeping him restrained. Crushing him.

A fiery black tongue slithered out of the demonic Holly's mouth and licked his cheek, searing off the flesh. The monstrous parody of Holly metamorphosed into Giovanni.

Kurt opened his mouth to scream, but no sound came out. His own scream filled up his throat, choking him.

With no further preamble, Kurt was torn from his body. His ascension dragged on for an eternity. The menace seeping from the ceiling filled him with increasing terror. Suddenly, he was only millimetres away from crossing that threshold.

With all his will, he tried to scream, to shake himself awake, to call out to Holly. The real Holly. He wondered if she was still alive. Or how long ago she might have been sacrificed to Giovanni's god.

And the image of that star from his childhood filled his mind—that rock Giovanni stole from him. He mourned the future it had promised him. He held on to that memory, made it glow as brightly as he could, believing it might be the only thing that could save him. But, despite himself, it dimmed until it became so dark he could not even remember what he was trying so hard to hold on to.

Giovanni laughed at him. Gloating.

As Kurt passed through the ceiling, dark tendrils wrapped themselves around him.

CHAPTER 5

Lost Girls

It's obvious to Sandra that Aydee feels like she doesn't belong here. Aydee, wrapped in layers of tattered and dirty clothes, wearing a tuque that tries hard to hide her face, fidgets nervously while she recounts the latest adventures of her "other self." Sandra begins to regret bringing her inside.

It's only midmorning; The Small Easy isn't very busy yet. Sandra—petite, extravagantly tattooed, fashionably underdressed—is sitting with Aydee at a table that looks out onto the street. Their muffins and coffee arrive. Sandra thinks the waitress is kind of cute: plump, friendly, frizzy-haired, sporting a nose ring.

Sandra expects Aydee to resume her story, but Aydee's attention has wandered. Russet—a brown mutt nearly as tall as a Great Dane but with the robust musculature of a Rottweiler—stares at her through the glass, one paw held up against the window. Aydee matches the dog's gesture.

There's a slight drizzle today, and the year's first hint of autumn chills the air. Sandra had insisted that they come inside. Aydee reluctantly agreed after Sandra suggested they could sit by the window to keep an eye on Russet. Aydee dislikes leaving him alone outside; even more so recently. Dogs are being found stabbed, murdered, and the city isn't doing anything about it.

Aydee sips her coffee silently, while Sandra thinks about today's story—some intricate yarn about Aydee's alter ego helping a group of time-lost prehistoric proto-humans find their deity, the Green Blue and Brown God—a primordial "god of life"—one among the several outlandish recurring characters in Aydee's fabrications. Sandra wants to prompt her to continue, but she hesitates. *Poor crazy Aydee and her crazy stories*, thinks Sandra, yet she's nevertheless fascinated by Aydee's imagination. Those weird stories of ancient tomes, powerful gods, and outrageous monsters excite Sandra— they sometimes seem more real to Sandra than her own dead-end life. She feels guilty about indulging, maybe even encouraging, Aydee in these delusions, but what else is she to do—ignore her?

As Aydee tells it, on the evening of her tenth birthday, she, hopelessly lonely and with nowhere to go, walked away from her abusive parents. She's been living on the street ever since. She believes that when she fell asleep in an alley that night, she was split into two people. The other Aydee had awoken to find herself rescued by a giant lioness—"the god of lost children"— only to be flung in the middle of an eternal conflict between the supposedly benevolent Green Blue and Brown God and Yamesh-Lot, a violent, amorphous god of darkness, which led her to discover a strange bookshop called Lost Pages. She ended up being more or less adopted by the shopkeeper, living with him and his many dogs, and apprenticing at the shop. Lost Pages is at the centre of Aydee's fantasy life, and Sandra's been seduced by the allure of this surreal bookshop: its inventory of arcane books that can't be found anywhere else; its knack for attracting—and helping—people (and other creatures) who are desperately lost.

Aydee breaks her muffin in two, slipping half of it into a coat pocket. "Gotta keep some for Russet," Aydee says, responding to Sandra's inquisitive stare, and then falls abruptly silent again.

Sandra feels selfish—she's already wolfed down her own muffin in three hurried mouthfuls—and wishes she could afford more food, but she barely has enough money to leave a tip. She should get a better-paying job, but together she and the boys make enough to get by; being a twenty-year-old high-school dropout with no special skills limits her options. Cleaning up the tattoo shop isn't exactly stimulating, but at least, in addition to the under-the-table slave wage, she gets her tattoos done free.

Recently she's been thinking of moving out on her own. For that she'd need more money, though. Tom's mood swings are getting worse all the time;

he's too focused on scoring drugs every night, and she's fed up with that scene. And, as sweet as Kevin can be to her, because of his paranoia about "strangers" they don't make other friends. It's the three of them against the world—only she doesn't believe that anymore.

She's never told them about Aydee; they would neither understand nor approve.

Some days, Aydee is cheerful, wrapped up in the magical life of her alter ego or simply enjoying Russet's company, but today Sandra can see that Aydee is having a rough time. She's distracted and nervous, and not just about leaving Russet outside.

Aydee starts crying. At first Sandra is too shocked to react, but then she reaches out and squeezes Aydee's wrist.

"Why did I wake up in that filthy alley? There's no Lost Pages. Not for me. I wish that other Aydee would come and rescue me. She's a hero, she really is. She helps people who think they have no place in the world find where they belong. I wish she'd be my hero. She runs Lost Pages now. She's strong and beautiful, with her hair braided and beaded and her skin as smooth as a baby's. Not like me." Aydee disentangles her wrist from Sandra's fingers and wipes her runny nose. "But we're still connected! I know everything that happens to her! She has to know about me! Why doesn't she come and find me, so I can be safe, too? Me and Russet. She has to find us some day. She has to!" Aydee glances outside at Russet, who is steadfastly focused on her. "It's getting cold again." She pauses. "I don't know if I can take another winter."

Not for the first time, Sandra wonders about Aydee's age. When she noticed her last February, begging on the street with her dog on the coldest day of the year, Sandra had assumed from her weathered face and scraggly voice that she must be around fifty. She's so frail and withered, but there's something about her features—the delicately small ears and nose, for example—that makes Sandra think Aydee might be closer to thirty, maybe even younger. Whenever Sandra asks, Aydee always answers, "Oh, I don't know. I've lost track."

The boys are sleeping off whatever shit was in the pills Tom brought home last night. To avoid them both, especially after that hateful quarrel, Sandra bunked on the couch, even though she hates sleeping alone.

In the bathroom, Sandra turns on the shower, waits for the water to get scalding hot, and then climbs in.

She knows that she should leave, that this relationship isn't working anymore, but where could she go? She's been with the boys for six years, since she met them at her first rave. The boys, already a couple by then, had seduced her as a joke—a *let's fuck the awkward, insecure virgin and make her cry* thing—but they ended up really liking her, and the three of them had become inseparable. Two years later, at sixteen, they ran away together, away from their intolerant families and from everyone else who claimed to know what was best for them.

As the steam soothes her, calms her, she watches her skin turn from olive to pink under the hot water. From the waist up, her entire body, including her face, is tattooed with stars, suns, moons, and planets of various sizes and shapes; dark green snakes coil upward from her ankles to bite her on the ass.

She's startled when Tom suddenly steps into the shower, followed by Kevin, who comes in from the opposite end. They both wince at the scalding water.

She feels vulnerable and threatened, her five-foot-three self sandwiched between these six-foot giants.

Kevin, behind her, presses down on her shoulders, his strong, dark fingers gently massaging her. Her back is so taut that even such mild pressure hurts.

Tom—of the quick temper and hateful words; of the tall, gaunt frame; of the eerily pale skin— is careful not to touch her. Looking at her with surprising tenderness, he says, "I'm sorry. I shouldn't talk to you that way. Not ever."

Sandra, emotionally exhausted, slumps against Kevin's firm, dark-brown flesh. He holds her and whispers her name. Tom steps toward them, enfolding both of them in his long arms. The tension drains from her, and she almost lets out a sob. Although she's squeezed tightly between the boys, she no longer feels trapped. She breathes in the musk of their smooth chests, breathes in the steam and the sweat, and she feels safe, at home, where she belongs, the only place she's ever belonged.

It's only late October, but a freak winter storm rages through the city. It's minus twenty degrees, with the wind-chill factor bringing it down another fifteen. According to the weather report, eighteen centimetres of snow have already fallen by three o'clock in the afternoon, with at least another thirty expected in the next twelve hours.

Sandra is consumed by worry about Aydee. As she piles on the layers and wraps scarves around her neck and head, she tells herself that it's stupid to go out in this storm—but she knows the pain in her gut won't go away unless she makes sure that her friend is safe. *Friend*. She's never thought about Aydee quite like that before today. For Sandra, Aydee has always been that crazy homeless lady with the dog. But Sandra realizes that, in fact, Aydee is her only friend. They spend time together almost every day, and Sandra has come to depend on the casual intimacy of their interactions.

Outside, Sandra instantly despairs. How will she ever find Aydee in this dark chaos of snow and wind? Sandra almost runs back in, but worry gnaws at her.

Calling out Aydee's name, Sandra walks toward The Small Easy, only two blocks away; Aydee usually loiters near that corner. In this weather, it takes Sandra almost fifteen minutes to walk there. She encounters no-one on the way, and neither is there anyone on the streets near the restaurant.

It occurs to her to check the alley. Aydee and Russet get most of their food from the dumpster out back, and its bulk can offer some degree of protection from the wind. The storm's getting fiercer, and Sandra knows that she'll have no choice but to give up the search soon.

She finds them there: Aydee and Russet huddled against each other, barely visible under a blanket of snow. Sandra gets in close and shouts against the wind, "Why aren't you in a shelter, Aydee? You can't stay outside on a day like this."

"Nobody'll let Russet in. I can't leave him alone. We always look out for each other. What kind of person would I be if I betrayed him? The other Aydee would never rescue someone like that."

"Aydee, you have to get inside. You could die out here, and then who would look out for Russet? Come on—come home with me."

"Can Russet come, too?"

Sandra thinks about the boys' obsessive tidiness, and Tom's need to be always in control. "No, the boys . . . they don't like dogs. They'd never allow it."

"Just go back home. We'll be fine, Russet and me. We'll keep each other warm."

Sandra can't bear the risk of losing her friend. She doesn't know how she'll make Kevin and Tom accept having Aydee, let alone Russet, in the apartment, but she'll have to find a way. She's freezing out here, and she just wants to get inside . . . but not without Aydee.

"Okay. Russet can come, too. Just hurry."

"No, we're staying right here. I don't want to go anywhere where we won't really be welcome. Don't worry about me. Just go home. I'll see you tomorrow, okay?"

"No! Not okay. Not okay at all. You have to come with me. Please. Please, come. For me. For Russet."

"Don't be patronizing. I'm not stupid." She looks away from Sandra, toward Russet. She rests a hand on his back, and he looks up at her—shivering. "But, okay, I'll come."

Sandra takes Aydee's hand, and runs home. Russet follows them.

It takes a bit of arguing, but Sandra convinces Aydee to take a hot bath. It's the bubblebath that did it, Sandra thinks; Aydee's eyes lit up when she mentioned that.

With Aydee sequestered in the bathroom, Russet has settled on the couch—the dog is so huge that it's almost too small for him—and no amount of coaxing on Sandra's part can get him down. It's going to be hard enough to convince the boys to let Aydee and Russet stay, but she knows it'll be impossible if they find the dog like this.

Maybe if she offered him food? He must be hungry—a big dog like that, with nothing but garbage to sustain him. She gets some chicken from the fridge and puts it in a plastic bowl. She places it on the floor, calling Russet's name. He sniffs the air, steps down from the couch, and trots over to the food.

Success!

But the dog grabs the meat in his mouth and saunters back to the couch, slobbering all over the upholstery as he eats. And that's when the boys walk in.

Soon after the yelling and the barking start, Aydee steps out of the bathroom—dripping wet in her dirty, tattered clothes. She calls Russet to her, and, without even glancing at Sandra, leaves.

Sandra yells at Aydee to stay, tries to run to her friend, but Tom grabs her.

Kevin shouts, "How dare you bring that street trash in here? And that filthy dog! They probably have lice and shit knows what else! What were you thinking? This is our home! It's not a zoo, for fuck's sake."

Sandra struggles free, but by that time Aydee and Russet are gone.

"How can you throw them out in weather like this? How can you be so cruel?"

Kevin says, "They're not our responsibility. We should rescue all the homeless people? There's no end to that if we start. We look out for each other, the three of us. Nobody else ever has; why the fuck should we give a damn about anyone else?"

"Because they're my friends!"

Tom says, "Why don't you go out there with them, then? Maybe that's where you really belong. With the dogs." His disgust is written all over his face.

Sandra remembers what Aydee said about never abandoning Russet, and she feels like a coward for not rushing out to join them. She runs into the bathroom and locks herself in, traps herself there.

She suddenly feels nauseous and throws up in the sink. While she cleans her face, she hears Tom say, "This cozy ménage with the fag hag has gone on long enough. We don't need her anymore. Fuck knows what other crap she does behind our backs."

Later, Kevin's voice comes through the bathroom door. "Sandy, baby. Look, I'm sorry things got so ugly. Tom knows he was way out of line. All we have is each other; we can't throw it all away because of a beggar and her dog."

Sandra doesn't say anything. All she can think about is that she let Aydee go out in that storm. She doesn't care about the boys anymore.

Kevin tries to cajole her for another ten minutes, but then he gives up. "Could you at least come out of there so we can use the can?"

Sandra does come out five minutes later, but she avoids the boys, doesn't say a word.

The boys go into the bathroom together; Kevin tells her they'll take a shower and then all three of them will talk later. She knows they'll use the noise of the shower to cover their conversation about her. Probably, they'll jerk each other off to calm themselves.

Sandra goes into the kitchen and throws some food in a bag: granola bars, raisins, things like that. From the bedroom closet, she grabs the biggest, thickest blanket she can find—an old, ratty quilt.

She puts on her winter gear and leaves.

Sandra's been out in the storm for hours. The cold has seeped into her bones. She can't find Aydee anywhere, and her legs hurt from overexhaustion. Visibility is much worse than before: she can't see farther than an arm's length; she's utterly lost.

She slips and falls. She loses the bag of food to the storm, but she manages to hold on to the quilt.

She doesn't have the strength to get up. Once more she yells, "Aydee!"—but the wind drowns her out.

She wraps herself in the quilt to take the edge off the wind. Within seconds, she's completely covered in snow. She tries to struggle free, but all her energy is spent and she loses consciousness.

The morning sunlight rouses her. The sky is cloud-free, and the wind has died down. It's much warmer—the snow around Sandra is moist, melting.

Sandra is astounded to be alive. She feels giddy, joyful.

She stands up. It hurts; her legs are stiff and cold.

Across the street, she sees a woman fiddling with the books in a store's window display. She looks up at the sign, green and blue letters painted onto a brown background: Lost Pages.

Inside the bookshop, Sandra is too nervous to face the woman. Browsing through the shelves, she notices that most of the books are in languages she can't even identify. Her eye falls on a tome whose jacket painting resembles her tattoos—twin snakes spiralling upward into the air against a backdrop of planets and stars—but she doesn't understand the strange script above the illustration.

She reaches out to pick up the book, but then she remembers why she's here. She looks up at the woman and blurts out, "You're Aydee," astonished at the sight of this clean and healthy version of her friend.

"Yeah, that's me. You looking for something in particular? Chances are we have it."

"I've walked down this street hundreds of times . . . I'm sure this store was never here before . . . I can't believe you're real. That this place is real."

Sandra had been right: her friend Aydee must have been younger than she appeared. Looking at this Aydee—a little taller than the Aydee she knows—Sandra can tell that she can't be more than twenty-five, maybe even only twenty. She's exactly like her friend described: long, braided hair; beautifully smooth creamy brown skin; strong shoulders.

"Don't tell me you're from one of those worlds where I'm a comic-book character or something. . . ." The bookseller lets out an irritated breath. "Look, you can click your heels all you want, but this place is real and so am I." She collects herself and continues in a friendlier tone. "Sorry. There's been a bit too much of that recently. Let's start over. . . . What can I do for you?"

Sandra looks around, and she's struck by a missing detail. "Where are the dogs? She always told me this place was full of dogs."

"She?" Aydee scrutinizes Sandra. "I've seen you . . ." Aydee shakes her head, and her eyes narrow suspiciously. "No, the dogs . . . I don't mind them, but that's always been more Lucas's thing. They're with him, and he's not here anymore. You know him?"

"I've heard about him."

There's an awkward silence.

Aydee says, "You're shivering. Do you want a cup of tea?"

Aydee sips her tea, listening quietly to Sandra's story.

Sandra repeats, "Say something. Do something. We have to help her. You have to find her. Save her."

Her voice simmering with anger, Aydee says, "I think you should leave."

"What?"

"Leave."

"But—"

Aydee gets out of her chair, grabs Sandra by the arm, pushes her outside, and locks the door to Lost Pages.

Sandra scours the neighbourhood for Aydee—her Aydee—while city trucks clean away the mountains of slush and snow. Sandra doesn't return to the apartment. After the storm, the temperature warmed up to above freezing, even at night. The quilt keeps her warm enough. She knows she should go to work, but she can't stomach the thought of cleaning up the mess at the tattoo parlour anymore. It's time for a change, even though she has no idea what that might entail. First, she has to find Aydee.

That other Aydee is no hero. My Aydee would never treat anyone like that. She's loyal and brave and strong of heart and . . .

A group of kids in the park—homeless ecopunks who hang out with a pack of dogs—say that they know Aydee and Russet, but they, also, have not seen either of them recently. The punks are mad about the dog stabber, about how the police aren't making any effort to solve the crimes. They've lost five of their dogs to the stabber in the last year; most recently, one was killed the day of the storm.

One of the girls—she can't be more than twelve—takes Sandra aside.

The girl whispers, "Do you have tampons or something? I'm bleeding."

"I think so. . . . Is this your first time?"

"Yeah."

As Sandra digs a handful of tampons out of her purse, she realizes that it's been more than two months since her last period.

That night, Sandra almost goes back to the boys—it's their baby, too—but in the end she decides it's better for everyone if the boys never know about this, better if she never sees them again. She's still not sure whether she's keeping the child or not. Probably not, though.

The last few days, Sandra has been too focused on finding Aydee to be afraid for her own safety. Now, realizing that she's pregnant, Sandra has become hyper-aware of her body and of its fragility.

She can't find a place to sleep. Everywhere there are men who look at her as if she were a piece of raw meat. She understands how vulnerable Aydee would have felt without Russet to guard her.

It's been almost a week, and there's still no sign of Aydee.

After yet another night during which she doesn't allow herself to sleep, Sandra hopes, now that the sun is up, she won't feel so much like prey.

She goes to the park where the ecopunks hang out during the day. Maybe she can nap next to them. They're nice kids. She wishes she knew where they went at night. Maybe she'll ask if she can tag along, at least for a while.

When they see her, the girl who asked about the tampons yesterday runs toward her, yelling, "Aydee's back!"

Sandra finds Aydee and Russet foraging in the dumpster behind The Small Easy. She hugs her friend. "I looked all over for you!"

"We hid out in that Greek place with the orange awning. It closed for a family emergency or something, and they didn't lock the back door properly. There was tons of food. Russet loved it! We hightailed it last night when we heard someone unlocking the front door."

Aydee extricates herself from Sandra.

"Plus, I stayed away because I was still ticked at you."

"I'm so sorry. I don't live there anymore. I . . ." Sandra doesn't know where to begin. Or what to say about the other Aydee, if anything at all.

Aydee cuts in, saying, "So you met her, huh? I know you used to think I was just this crazy lady, but you were nice to me anyway. You always listened."

Sandra is shocked. "Did you meet her, too?"

"No. I told you, I know everything that happens to her, and now she's very angry, very confused. All these years, she thought that my life was just a nightmare that haunted her: her worst fears of how her life would have turned out if the lioness hadn't intervened. She's terrified that her whole life is a fantasy. That only I'm real. It'll be better for her if we never meet."

"But I thought you wanted her to save you?"

"No . . . I was wrong about that. I've got my own life. And I've got Russet. We do well together." Aydee laughs, opening her arms to let Sandra in. "And we have each other too, now, right?"

In Sandra's dream, she and Aydee are playing with her child—she's not sure if it's a boy or a girl—in a big park full of dogs, including Russet. Everyone is happy and playful. Russet rushes up to her and licks her face. He steps back and barks, then licks her again. He does this several times until Sandra wakes up to the real Russet's tongue on her face.

In the dark, she reaches out to pet him, and her hand falls on something sticky. Sandra immediately thinks of the dog stabber and knows that this is blood. She shouts, "Aydee! Russet is hurt! Aydee!" Where is she? The last thing Sandra remembers before going to sleep is resting her head in Aydee's lap right here next to the dumpster.

The dog starts running; Sandra has no choice but to follow. She's not fast enough for him, so he keeps having to stop and run back to her to make sure she's following.

Russet reaches Aydee, who's on the ground, leaning against the wall of an alley. He whines desperately, kissing her face, darting quick, worried glances at Sandra. She realizes that Russet isn't covered in his own blood.

There's blood pooling around Aydee; she's holding a hand against her ribs. She holds Sandra's gaze and says, "Take me to her."

"Her? Who? . . . That other Aydee? No! I have to get you to a hospital."

Aydee coughs blood. "Too weak to argue. Do as I say. Please. She knows we're coming. Knows what to do."

Sandra is anxious to get Aydee looked at by a doctor, but she doesn't dare betray her friend's wishes again. As Sandra kneels down to wrap Aydee's right arm around her shoulders, she sees a man lying face up on the ground next to the opposite wall.

There's just enough light for her to see that his throat is ripped open. Next to his chewed-up right hand, there's a bloody dagger.

Weakly, Aydee says, "Russet had run off. I found him—" Aydee coughs again, and Sandra winces at the pain on her friend's face. Aydee continues in a whisper: "Guy was giving him steak while pulling a knife on him. I screamed. Ran to save Russet. Guy stabbed me. Then Russet got him."

The other Aydee is waiting for them outside the door to Lost Pages. When she sees them, she rushes over and helps Sandra carry the wounded and barely conscious Aydee into the shop.

Russet sniffs the other Aydee. His tail perks up, wagging enthusiastically, and he runs rings around the three women.

Inside, the other Aydee says, "This is my fault. If only I'd . . ."

Sandra doesn't trust this Aydee. Her Aydee is going to die, and she's powerless to prevent it. Unable to keep the anger out her voice she says, "So, how are you going to save her? She always told me you were a hero. But you're just a coward."

Before the Lost Pages Aydee can reply, the wounded Aydee opens her eyes and says, "It's you. It's really you." Blood gurgles out of her mouth; she coughs, spitting out more blood.

The other Aydee says, "Yes." Tears stream down her face.

The blood-stained Russet sniffs both Aydees intently.

The Lost Pages Aydee pulls a pendant from under

her shirt. The palm-sized jewel reflects shades of green, blue, and brown. She clasps it in the wounded Aydee's hand, then enfolds that hand with both of hers. She bends down, brushing her face against her doppelganger's. She opens her mouth and kisses her double's bloody lips and . . .

. . . green, blue, and brown light explodes into the bookshop.

Sandra loses all sense of herself; she experiences life—simultaneously, chaotically, blissfully—through the bodies of countless creatures: flying in strange skies, swimming through primordial oceans, worshipping monstrous deities, smelling alien flowers, hunting elusive prey, hiding from ravenous predators, giving birth to a litter of exotic animals . . .

As the Godlight fades, Sandra feels that a lifetime of ignored wounds have been healed. With calm joy she looks at Russet licking the other Aydee's hand. But panic rises within her when she notices that her Aydee has disappeared.

Sandra screams, "Where is she? What have you done to her?"

There are tears on Aydee's face. She moves closer and opens her mouth, but she seems unable to speak.

Baring her teeth in fury, Sandra pushes her away. Then Aydee erupts with laughter, crying even harder. "Sandra, it's me! It's both of us. We're one person again. Finally."

Aydee lifts her shirt, and there are fading scars where she'd been stabbed. Sandra looks at her face, and it's true: the new Aydee's face is a composite of both their faces, not as worn as the one, not as smooth as the other.

Aydee says it's good to have a dog in the bookshop again. It amuses her when Russet intimidates customers by following them around.

These strange books about secret histories, lost worlds, and weird gods; the otherwordly clientele; the tenuous connection with any one reality— Sandra's fascinated by it all, and amazed that she's really working at Lost Pages.

As Sandra leafs through the book whose cover painting bears a curious resemblance to her tattoos—

admiring the ornate hand-drawn illuminations but still unable to decipher the writing—she hears Russet snore from the foot of the bed. She yawns, puts the heavy tome aside, and gently presses her hands against the not-so-subtle bulge of her belly.

Sandra blows out the candle. She lies down and spoons Aydee.

The Daily Star, November 15
News Briefs, page A7

The body of the heavily tattooed young Caucasian woman discovered wrapped in a quilt on Green Avenue in the aftermath of the freak snow storm that hit the city in late October has still not been identified. The coroner's office has found no evidence of foul play and has concluded that hypothermia was the cause of death. The young woman was pregnant.

CODA

The Lost and Found of Years

Phone rings. It's Jasper. Says he wants a Montreal story for a new anthology he's preparing, something about cities. Go crazy, he says.

Big money, he says. Hard/soft deal with Knopf/Vintage. HBO planning mini-series based on his concept, adapting stories from his book for TV. Put in all the sex you want, he tells me. It's cable TV. Money, he says again.

Right. Money. But any of it for me? I ask.

Tell Jasper about Bestial Acts deal. The first story about my fictional bookshop, Lost Pages. Haynes bought the rights, made a film with Depp playing Lucas. Big indie hit. Didn't see a dime. Not even a penny. Pringle took it all. Read your contract, he said. Fucking publishers.

Tell Jasper I'll think about it.

Money sounds like a good thing. No story ideas, though.

Take the dog out for a walk. Look around. Maybe something in the neighbourhood will spark an idea or two.

Girlfriend always says I never notice anything. Always in my head. Stores go out of business. New buildings go up. And I'm just clueless.

I'm not really that bad. But she's not wrong, either.

Walk around with the dog, look at stuff. But I get no story ideas.

Long walk, though. Makes the dog happy, at least.

Girlfriend says, Take that camera I got you for your

birthday last year. You know, the one you never use. Take pictures of the neighbourhood. It'll rev up your imagination. You'll think up a story in no time.

Yeah, right.

I go out with the dog again. And the camera.

Meet lots of people from the neighbourhood. Portuguese grandmothers who can speak neither French nor English. Cute McGill students. Other dog walkers. Clerks from the neighbourhood bakeries, the newsstand, the used bookstores. People who know me 'cause they see me walk the dog all the time.

They all fuss over the dog. They always do.

Dog just soaks it all in. Wags his tail. Smiles. Pants.

I don't manage to shoot any pictures. No inspiration. Getting depressed. Go to the park to play with the dog.

Betcha Jasper never thought about how happy his stupid anthology would make my dog.

Lots of dogs in the park. Dog loves it. Humps a bunch of them.

Fuck it, I'm too depressed. Can't play anymore. Head back home. Dog's not too happy about leaving the park.

Girlfriend gives me a good pep talk. We gab about Montreal. What's fun about it. What's special about it.

All the different kinds of people. Culturally diverse. No violence. People holding hands and kissing in public. Gay. Straight. Whatever. Lots of sexy girls. Great city to walk around in twenty-four hours a day. Easy to make friends. And the food. People love eating. All kinds of food. And bakeries everywhere. Bagels. Croissants. Baguettes. More.

Then, bad stuff. The paranoid Anglos who think their culture is threatened. Yeah, right. The gullible Francophones who believe all that tripe about being oppressed. Yeah, right.

Nowhere near as many people like that as the media makes it appear. Most people just like to get along. Québécois. Anglos. Jews. Arabs. Blacks. Asians. Latinos. Whatever.

More bad stuff. Everyone fucking smokes. Well,

not everyone, but, fuck, it sure feels like it sometimes. And everyone's always late. Always. Montreal
custom. Hate that.

Well, so what. Still no ideas for a story.

Fuck.

Temperature shoots up ten degrees today. The sky is
clear, and the sun is hot. It's just a few degrees above
freezing, but, for us Montrealers, so eager to leave
winter behind, it's like the first taste of summer.

Go out to Rue St-Denis with the girlfriend.

Same as every year on the first day with even a
hint of spring. All the terraces are open for business.
Everyone eating outside, everyone underdressed,
everyone checking each other out, everyone happy
and chatty.

Fuck, there's a lot of beautiful girls in this city.
And it's nice to see a bit of flesh again, after months
of winter.

Girlfriend notices me noticing.

She laughs. She always does.

I love it when she laughs.

She gives me that look. I love that look.

We go home and fuck. We have so much fun we can't stop laughing, even while we're cumming.

Still no idea for a story, though.

I decide to try again with the camera. I don't bring the dog this time. I give him a cookie instead. He takes it in his mouth and plops himself on the couch.

Okay. I'm outside. I've got the camera.

Take pictures. Lots of pictures. Old school. With film.

Buildings. Skylines. People. Dogs. Trees. Stuff on the ground.

Run out of film pretty fast. Fun, though.

Dunno if it'll help me with the story or not.

I go buy more rolls of film. Lots more. What the hell.

I feel good.

I go home and write.

I write a whole story in one sitting. But it has nothing to do with Jasper's anthology.

I reread my new story. I'm pretty happy with it. Needs only a bit of editing. A big turning point in my Lost Pages mythology. I send it off to Klima at *Electric Velocipede*.

I try the camera thing again. Use up another whole roll. Fun.

But no new story ideas today. Not for Jasper, and not for anything else.

I do the camera thing every day now. Sometimes I bring the dog, but it's too distracting.

I end up taking lots of walks. Camera walks; and dog walks. I try to leave enough time for writing.

Story for Jasper. Book for Savory. Novella for Kasturi.

Today, I notice something weird. But it's too freaky. I'll look at the pictures again tomorrow. Probably too tired. Seeing things.

Halpern on the phone. Wants a new Lost Pages story for a Di Filippo tribute anthology.

I ask about the money.

Print on demand, he says. No money up front, but higher royalties. Royalties. Yeah, right.

I tell him I'll think about it.

In bed. Trying to sleep. Girlfriend snoring. It's kinda cute. Makes me smile. But restless anyway.

Didn't use the camera today. Dog walks only. Didn't write anything.

Didn't look at the pictures.

Don't want to deal with it. Too weird.

Can't get to sleep. Get up. Go look at the pictures.

I look at the pictures. Of the row of houses across the street from our house. I spread them on my desk. Compare them. And there it is. I can't deny it.

I look out the window of my office. Across the street. To that house.

And there it is.

Fuck.

Should I wake her up? Fuck. That makes her grumpy. She'd bite my head off.

I'm gonna wait till morning.

Go back to bed.

Try to sleep.

Can't sleep. I have to tell someone. Show someone.

I whisper girlfriend's name. Touch her shoulder.

She mumbles. Doesn't really wake up.

I try harder. Say her name. Once. Twice. Little shake.

She mumbles again and turns away from me.

I shake her harder. Say her name and, You have to wake up. I need to talk to you.

She turns toward me. Opens her eyes. She's not happy.

She gets up. Reluctantly. Puts on a T-shirt.

Dog lifts his head to see what's going on, but then he moves around and settles on my pillow.

I drag the girlfriend into my office.

She is annoyed, but not biting my head off.

Good.

She can tell that I'm really upset. Takes it seriously. Takes me seriously.

I show her.

Look, I say. Look. Look.

I point to that house, on a whole bunch of different photos.

She doesn't get it.

She says, It's that house across the street. So what?

I say, Don't you notice something weird?

She doesn't get it.

I drag her to the window. I point to the house across the street.

Look. Look!

I hold a picture of that row of houses in each hand. Pictures from two different days.

Look at these. Then look outside. That house. There! Don't you see?

No, she doesn't.

Fuck.

Why the fuck did you wake me up, she says. Is this another of your stupid jokes, she says.

No.

We fight.

It gets ugly.

She gets dressed and storms out of the house.

I shouldn't have woken her up.

Okay. Calm down.

Fuck. Fuck. Fuck.

Stupid house.

Fuck you, stupid fucking house across the street.

Girlfriend always says I don't notice anything.

But now she's the one not noticing.

Not seeing. But why not?

Fuck. This is too weird. Plus, she's mad at me.

I hate it when we fight.

This is all Jasper's fault. Stupid fucking anthology.

Okay. Calmer now.

I look at the pictures again.

Then I look at the house.

Fuck.

Every day, it's a different house.

Every day, that house changes.

It's not the same house from one day to the next.

Okay. Stop reiterating. No matter how I say it, it still sounds crazy.

One day, it's a well-kept red-brick duplex.

The next, it's a triplex, with one of those famous Montreal outdoor staircases.

And then, it becomes an ugly 1970s apartment building, with half the windows boarded up.

And then, a gorgeous old-fashioned place with big, grey stonework.

Then, a yuppy townhouse.

Then, a croissanterie.

A travel agency.

A condo development.

A pet shop.

An empty lot.

A small park with nice big trees and a couple of benches.

A narrow renovated house with a driveway on the side, in the same style as ours.

I look out the window again.

Right now, it's a barber shop.

Can't sleep.

Get dressed. Go for a nighttime walk with the dog.

He growls at me when I get him out of bed. By

the time we're outside he's happy enough. Wagging. Running. Sniffing.

I do not look at the house across the street.

Breakfast. I make pancakes. Sausages. With maple syrup. Girlfriend is back. Not talking to me. But sits with me while we eat. So things not too bad.

Tea for her. Orange juice for me.

I don't mention the house.

I don't say anything.

We eat.

She has to go to work.

She almost gives me a hug.

Stops herself.

Then hugs me anyway.

Okay. Things are good.

I decide to never mention that house again.

When I sit at my desk, I can see that house through the window.

Today, it's a teepee.

Maybe I should move my office around. So I don't see outside while I work.

I stare out the window all the time. I try to see the house change. To witness that moment of transformation.

Fuck.

I always miss it.

I go to the bathroom. I yawn and blink for a second too long. Whatever.

I always miss it.

Changes getting weirder. Bizarre architectures. Foreign. Or something.

One night, I recognize it. From one of my stories. Not a house that time. But a vast, dark, deep hole in the ground, surrounded by a moat of water sparkling with green, blue, and brown light. Giant black tendrils erupt savagely from the hole in the ground, kept in check by the godly waters.

Too weird.

Not sleeping. Not writing.

Fuck.

Midnight. Can't sleep. Girlfriend and dog curled up together, sleeping. They're beautiful.

Get up.

The house looks kind of futuristic tonight.

I'm so fucking tired.

Peculiar architecture. All curves and unusual angles. Don't recognize the building material. Some kind of stone, but different. Weird.

Window slides open. Woman appears.

Naked. At least the part of her I can see.

Dark wavy hair to her shoulders. Light brown skin. Big eyes. Full lips. Svelte with soft curves. Full, firm, round breasts. Looks about twenty.

She notices me looking. Staring.

She laughs.

I love it when girls laugh.

She turns away for a second and gestures with her hand.

A second woman joins her.

They look exactly the same. Twins?

They laugh.

I love it when they laugh.

They touch each other's breasts, looking at me.

I'm so hard I feel like a teenager.

They gesture for me to come join them.

On my way out I see the dog and my girlfriend on the bed. Sleeping.

I should stay here. I love her. She loves me.

I go outside.

The women are still at the window.

They're the most beautiful girls I've ever seen. They look at me. Gesture for me come to them.

Fuck, I'm almost creaming just thinking about them.

I walk to the house. To the door. Strange futuristic door. Have no idea how to open it.

While I try to figure it out, it dissolves. And I see inside.

And the girls are there, on the floor. Naked. Looking at me with their mouths open just so.

Fuck, they're gorgeous.

And then I think: What happens if the house changes while I'm in there? Will I vanish along with it? To another place?

With these girls.

But I love my girlfriend. And she loves me.

I hear the girls moan.

I'm trembling. My cock is almost ripping through my pants.

I look at them. They're a fantasy.

I run back home.

Wake up girlfriend. Dog growls and jumps out of bed.

Take my clothes off. Kiss girlfriend. Have sex. I cum right away. But then I make her cum once, twice, three times. I love her.

I sleep for fifteen hours.

Lying in bed, waking up. I feel so good.

Then, phone call from Jasper. How's the story coming along?

I lie.

Phone rings again. Kasturi. Where's that Lost Pages novella I promised her?

I lie.

Phone rings again. Savory needs to know when I'll hand in the manuscript. Book's listed in the new catalogue, he reminds me.

The phone. Again. Halpern. Still wants a new Lost Pages story for that Di Filippo book.

Fuck.

I haven't written anything for months. Way behind.

I don't feel so good anymore.

Step out the door, walking dog.

It's not a house across the street today.

It's a lush garden, with a giant apple tree in the middle. With a naked man and a naked woman. They kind of look Jewish, except that the guy isn't circumcised.

They're contemplating the apple tree.

There's a snake slithering around. A luminous, seductive snake.

This is too weird.

Girlfriend says she's worried about me. I seem troubled, distracted. Asks about my writing.

We fight. It gets real ugly. She storms out.

I know it's my fault.

Fuck.

Today, the house is a bookshop.

Not just any bookshop.

Lost Pages. The bookshop from my stories.

The stuff my dreams are made of. Cliché, but true.

I walk up to it. I peer through the window.

Inside, a man and a girl in her teens. Lucas and Aydee. My characters. Me.

I haven't written anything for months.

I hear barking.

I look back toward my house. My dog is looking at me through my office window. Barking at me. Telling me to come back.

I think about my girlfriend. I love her.

She loves me.

I haven't written anything for months.

I open the door to Lost Pages and step inside.

Acknowledgements

Portions of *The Door to Lost Pages* have previously appeared, in different form, in *Interzone* #178 (April 2002); *OtherDimension.com* (July 2002); *Interzone* #186 (February 2003); *Intracities* (Unwrecked Press 2003), edited by Michael Jasper; *SDO Fantasy* (April 2004); and *The Mammoth Book of Best New Erotica 4* (Robinson 2005), edited by Maxim Jakubowski.

About the Author

Claude Lalumière (lostmyths.net/claude) is the author of the story collection *Objects of Worship* (ChiZine Publications 2009) and the chapbook *The World's Forgotten Boy and the Scorpions from Hell* (Kelp Queen Press 2008). He has edited eight anthologies, including the Aurora Award nominee *Tesseracts Twelve: New Novellas of Canadian Fantastic Fiction* (Edge 2008), and he writes the Fantastic Fiction column for *The Montreal Gazette*. With Rupert Bottenberg, Claude is the co-creator of Lost Myths, which is both a live show and an online archive updated weekly at lostmyths.net.

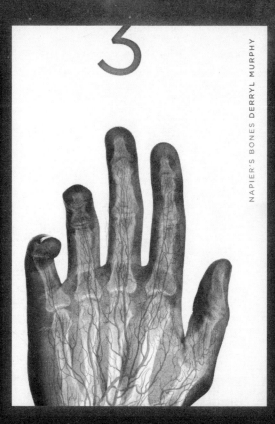

NAPIER'S BONES DERRYL MURPHY

COMING MARCH 15, 2011
FROM CHIZINE PUBLICATIONS

978-1-926851-10-5

EVERY
SHALLOW
CUT
TOM
PICCIRILLI

COMING MARCH 15, 2011
FROM CHIZINE PUBLICATIONS

978-1-926851-10-5

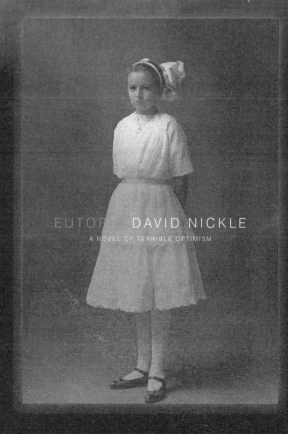

EUTOPIA **DAVID NICKLE**

A NOVEL OF TERRIBLE OPTIMISM

COMING APRIL 15, 2011
FROM CHIZINE PUBLICATIONS

978-1-926851-11-2

A ROPE OF THORNS

GEMMA FILES

VOLUME TWO OF THE HEXSLINGER SERIES

COMING MAY 15, 2011
FROM CHIZINE PUBLICATIONS

978-1-926851-14-3

978-0-9812978-9-7

978-0-9812978-8-0

978-0-9812978-7-3

TIM LEBBON

PHILIP NUTMAN

SIMON LOGAN

THE THIEF OF BROKEN TOYS

CITIES OF NIGHT

KATJA FROM THE PUNK BAND

978-0-9812978-6-6

978-0-9812978-5-9

978-0-9812978-4-2

GEMMA FILES

DOUGLAS SMITH

NICHOLAS KAUFMANN

A BOOK OF TONGUES

CHIMERASCOPE

CHASING THE DRAGON

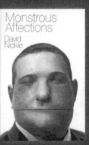

EMBRACE

THE

ODD

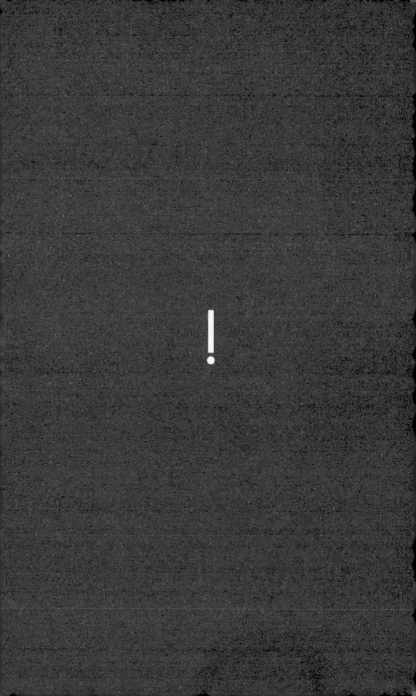

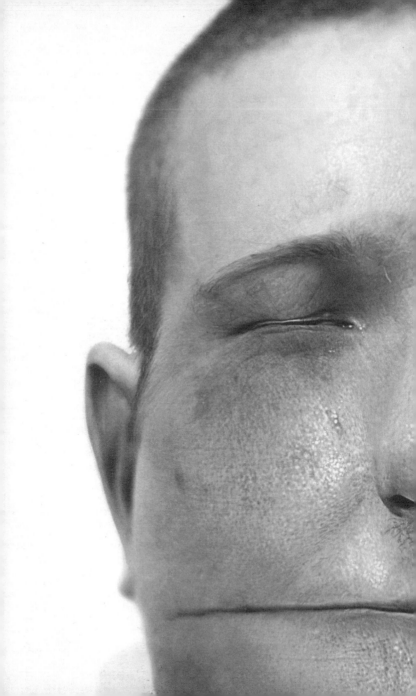

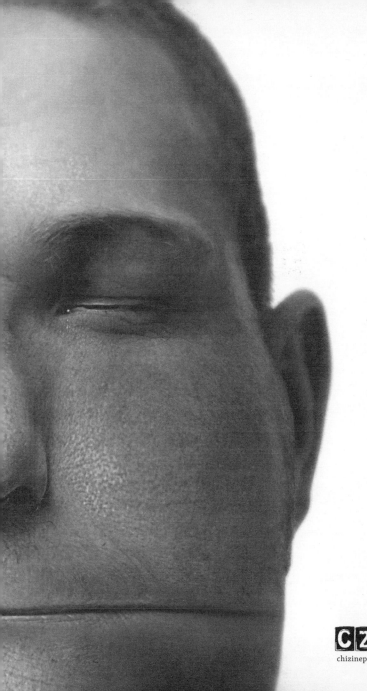